DAV

David Armstron
1946.

After leaving school at mixteen, he worked as a
salesman, building labourer, lorry-driver, and
sold books to the British Forces in Germany.

In 1974, after taking a degree at the University
of Wales, Cardiff, he began teaching at a College
of Further Education in Shropshire.

Less Than Kind is his second novel; his first,
Night's Black Agents, was shortlisted for 1993 John
Creasey Award for Best First Crime Novel of the
Year.

DAVID ARMSTRONG

Less Than Kind

'A little more than kin, and less than kind!'
Hamlet

HarperCollins*Publishers*

HarperCollins*Publishers*
77–85 Fulham Palace Road,
Hammersmith, London W6 8JB

This paperback edition 1995
1 3 5 7 9 8 6 4 2

First published in Great Britain by
HarperCollins*Publishers* 1994

ISBN 0 00 649009 3

Set in Baskerville

Printed in Great Britain by
HarperCollinsManufacturing Glasgow

For Jesse and Hannah

CHAPTER ONE

The only woman that Ieuwan Hopkins had ever seen naked was his wife. They had been married fourteen years and her body no longer gave him the thrill or excitement of surprise and novelty.

Usually, when he looked down from Ty Uchaf farm across his fields, he saw only ewes and magpies, crows and cattle, the familiar hedgerow trees of oak and ash, and the rutted strip of metalled lane that wound down to the valley floor. The most arresting thing that was likely to catch his eye was a skulking fox, making its stealthy progress along the hedges towards its prey at dusk.

Amid these changeless changes, the sight of the young woman washing herself at the tap outside Well Cottage two hundred yards away thrilled him deeply.

His first instinct was to rush into the kitchen and share the revelation with Glenys. His second was to stay alone, concealed beside the old barn. He stayed.

The young woman lathered herself in the cold water: her breasts, under her arms and down to her waist. She brought the soap and water on to her and shirked its cold all in one motion. Then she soaked the flannel and washed the soap from herself. As she bent closer to the tap her breasts swayed and Ieuwan's member grew huge against his leg.

She washed between her legs and then began to dry herself with the towel that was hung on the little brass handle of the white-painted wooden door. And that was it. She turned, the big towel draped about her, looked up the fields that sloped away from the cottage, and stepped back inside.

*

When they had arrived from London on a chill March evening a few weeks ago, Cyril Liptrot, the landlord of the Horseshoe Inn, had driven them from the village up the steep lanes to see his deserted cottage. It lay forty yards from the pool of still, black water from which, perhaps two hundred years ago, it had taken its name.

James and Susie had stood at the door with the publican and his panting labrador, and enthusiastically agreed to take the place at a peppercorn rent, the only proviso being that they keep the roof slates on and the guttering and downspouts free of leaves.

In front of the cottage, beyond the rough grass with its two damson trees and gnarled pear, ran a fast stream just wide enough for a man to jump. The tufty grass sprouted bunches of big daffodils that had been left to multiply undisturbed for many years. A ewe grazed in the unfenced garden and bleated to the dusk. The plaintive response of its lamb came from across the fast water and the mother scuttled away towards it.

Behind the little house was a wooded hill that inclined sharply before being dwarfed itself by a bracken-covered Montgomeryshire mountain. That evening, as the light faded behind Pentrefelin Hill, the crows in the wood disputed loudly as they circled the tops of the trees and peered down at the new residents.

Excited and tired and slightly afraid of the blackness that descended all around them, they tumbled their belongings out of the Bedford van and into the stone cottage. They slept that night on their mattress on the slate floor, a fire of crackling dry sticks in the hearth.

Glenys Hopkins never did find out why her previously torpid sex life became increasingly frenetic that spring. But she was not unhappy to receive once more the carnal attentions of her ruddy husband, even though he was a little rough with her in his graceless way.

For his part, the hill farmer spent each morning beside the black barn awaiting the careful ablutions of their new neighbour.

Humphreys-the-post told the locals that the new couple were 'come from London', he had been invited into the cottage and drunk tea with them as he brought the first of many envelopes. The comely woman had made him feel welcome and filled his cup and offered him biscuits from a tin. At his own home, in the next village, it was well known that he was not allowed to set foot upon the hall carpet without first removing his shoes.

In Well Cottage, he sat at the hearth in the couple's one big armchair, and was made to feel an honoured visitor. This did not endear them to him (they were foreigners, immigrants whose inept hospitality was born of a kind of remarkable ignorance), but rather focused his resentment against his own mean-spirited people, people who never asked you in, no matter how wet and cold you were as you cycled up the hill with their bank statements and farming catalogues.

The single-storey, random-stone cottage had been empty since Jack Lewis and his wife had moved down to the village five years ago. The vegetable garden that Jack had dug deep and fed well during many evenings had been lost in the first full year. The rich, dark loam became a bed of thistles and convolvulus that rapidly colonized the fertile soil. The ground elder spread its creamy, brittle tendrils beneath the earth, and the nettles and dandelions shed their copious seed. By autumn, apart from a rogue potato tuber and a few leggy sprout plants, thinnings not worth the taking to his new patch, it was as if Jack and quiet Mrs Lewis had never been there.

For the next five years the cottage became just another part of the natural landscape that Ieuwan Hopkins had always known. The trees had their seasons; one year the walnut in the middle field had good leaf and heavy crop; the next, the cherry blossom came early and was soon shaken; the same year, the lambs dropped in the mild weather but then many were lost in the perilous wet.

And Well Cottage, tucked amongst the fruit trees in the bottom field, glistened in the April rain, baked slowly in the July sun, and was lost in the still, deadening silence of February's blanket of snow.

Mice scurried about inside and ate the piece of soap and stubs of candle that Mrs Lewis had left on the kitchen window-sill. Outside, as the nails rusted, slates slipped and fell; more were lifted in the big October winds.

One year, the cast-iron guttering parted from the barge-board beneath the weight of thawing snow, and from that day on rain-water gathered in a pool beneath the break.

Liptrot, the rubicund publican, rarely visited his cottage. He had bought the place from Colonel Philip Somerville eight years previously. The Colonel had let it be known that he was thinking of selling 'one or two of the cottages on the estate'.

His manner was cavalier, even dismissive: he owned several upland farms, and hundreds of Montgomeryshire acres had been in the Somerville family for generations; but the fact was, the farms were tenanted for life, and the Montgomeryshire acres were on thin, stony soil that grew poor grass and worse corn.

Even here, in these distant hills, the proselytizing of trades union leaders had eventually percolated: labour costs escalated, while the death duties that the Somerville Estate had been obliged to pay to a post-war government on the death of Philip Somerville's father had taken virtually all of the remaining capital.

Notwithstanding these inconveniences, Somerville maintained a small stable of thoroughbreds, rode out to hounds, drove a huge Rover saloon, and lived, a mile outside Llantrisillio, in big, draughty, costly-to-maintain Plas Trisillio Hall.

It was common knowledge in the village that the marmalade on the kitchen table at the Hall was long gone before the local shop was paid for it; and the wheat stood four inches high in the flat fields that fronted the river before the agricultural merchant eventually received payment for his seed. In recent years, it had only been through the sale of a cottage here, a parcel of land there, or a stand of beech to the timber merchant, that the trades-people had been paid at all.

Cyril Liptrot, landlord of the quaint and profitable Horseshoe Inn, erstwhile sergeant in a Staffordshire infantry regiment, emasculated by the land-owning Colonel's birth and rank and very vowels, felt rather smug. He made the Colonel an offer for Well Cottage. It was a derisory offer, calculated to slight the man.

Philip Somerville accepted it by letter through his solicitors in London the following week.

Liptrot was a man of property; and, for that month at least, the garage and the seedsman and the village shop were paid their overdue accounts by the penurious Colonel.

CHAPTER TWO

Young Charles Somerville left London before dawn and drove north-west through the April morning: High Wycombe, Oxford, Cheltenham and across to Ledbury. From Hereford on the A49, parallel to the Welsh border, and never more than a few miles from it, he wound all the way up into rolling Shropshire.

Near Chirbury, he crossed first Offa's Dyke and then the River Severn into Wales. At Llanfrynach, where the Tanat, the Vyrnwy and the Trisillio all meet, he lumbered across the old pack bridge, and arrived at Len Hughes's yard outside Llanarmon just after eleven o'clock.

Hughes, a mechanic with doubtful credentials, bought and sold cars. He had a string of petty motoring convictions: bald tyres, no motor insurance, driving without a current excise licence. But his most recent offence had merited nearly half a page in the *Welshpool Recorder*: he had been convicted of taking thirty thousand miles off the clock of a middle-aged Austin Mini, and thereby putting on to its sale price about one hundred and fifty pounds.

'Clocking' cars was common enough in 1968, but detection was less likely in the middle of Manchester or Birmingham than it was in a village on the Welsh borders. Unfortunately for Len, the previous owner of the car met the new one only a fortnight later at Welshpool livestock market. After chatting about the price of store cattle, tups and barren ewes, the desultory conversation turned to second-hand cars.

They wandered over to the car park and stood beside the red Mini. It looked well. It had had a little bit of touching up done to the rusty spots on the bodywork in a colour that almost matched the original, and the tyres had been given a coat of black tyre paint which lent them a new appearance. But it wasn't on the appearance alone that the farm labourer had bought the little car, it was on its 'genuine low mileage', as guaranteed by the seller, Len Hughes.

Len was fined seventy-five pounds and given a suspended sentence by the magistrates' court one Friday morning. The chairman of the bench gave a stern admonition and told him that they didn't want to see him before them again. By lunch-time Len was back at his yard and welding together the chassis of an insurance write-off that he had bought in Llanidloes the previous weekend.

Charles drove in past the hand-painted sign, Llanarmon Motors. At the sound of the approaching car, Len turned down the Everley Brothers on his record player and came out of the stone cottage that abutted his corrugated iron workshop.

Even before he had taken in the appearance of the driver, his practised eye was surveying the Austin 1100 that pulled up in front of him, its front wheel lurching into a deep, oily puddle.

Somerville clambered out. 'Good morning. Is it Len? Len Hughes?'

Len knew the gangly young man by sight, but he had never spoken to him. The youth had an ungainly lack of co-ordination that the hulking mechanic associated with the upper classes.

'I'm Len. What do you want?' The question sounded more like a threat.

Undaunted, the boy replied, 'I'm Charles. Philip Somerville's son.' With his hands in his pockets, he shifted his weight from foot to foot, appeared unable to keep still. 'I'm getting rid of this. I wondered how much you'd give me for it?'

'What's wrong with it?' asked Len as he began a slow progress around the car.

'There's nothing wrong with it. I've got a new car lined up and I need the cash from this one. It's a cash deal. No part exchange.'

Maybe, thought Len. He'd heard it all before. He never believed a word anyone told him about cars. *He* never told the truth. Why should anyone else? But he asked the questions just the same. It didn't tell you anything about the car, but it told you a bit about the person you were dealing with. Like what was this tall, fair-haired boy in blue jeans and a checked shirt doing in his yard at eleven o'clock in the morning trying to sell him a car. And him not just some ordinary kid from the village, but a boy with what his mother had used to call 'breeding'.

The car itself was all right, and he almost certainly owned it. It wasn't that kind of set-up. But why was he selling it here? You could sell a car in the paper, or to a proper dealer. Len had no illusions about himself. There must be a reason. There always was.

He put his unlaced boot up on the front wheel and gave it a firm, steady push.

'What do you want for it?'

'What's it worth?' replied Somerville.

'What it's worth and what I'm offering may not be the same.'

'Well, what are you offering?' The boy was aware of the bit of sham theatre that the situation demanded, but he lacked the patience for the ritual.

Len knew a straight car when he saw one, and this car was straight. It had been washed recently, not very well; the ashtray was overflowing and there were cigarette packets and papers and junk on the floor. But with rich people, what you saw what you got. They couldn't be bothered hiding things and patching them up and trying to pull the wool over your eyes. In fact, they always thought the car was worse than you did: they had no idea how a good tidy-up would transform it.

'I'll give you two-fifty.'

It was about a hundred and fifty less than the car was worth.

'Make it three hundred,' said the boy.

Len responded according to the well-worn script. 'I'll split the difference; two-seven-five.'

Charles extended his hand in agreement. 'I'd like cash, if that's all right with you.'

As the man offered his grimy hand, Charles added, 'Would you run me up to the house? I've got a bit of stuff in the boot.'

Len went into the cottage, turned off his gramophone player and returned with the five-pound notes. He locked his front door, got into the driver's seat of the 1100 and reversed out on to the lane that led to Llantrisillio four miles away.

CHAPTER THREE

'Do you fancy a bit of sheep-shagging?'

Munroe ignored Superintendent Glover and walked on into the locker-room. Glover followed.

'Seriously. Do you fancy an away day? Get to know our country cousins?'

'Why? What's up?' Inspector John Munroe had no stomach for banter. He'd been lying concealed in the back of a Ford Corsair all night waiting for some robbers who never came. He was exhausted. He ached everywhere. His teeth were unclean. He was unshaven. He'd been hoping to see the Villa play at home today. They were playing Birmingham City. It should be a good game. And now all he wanted to do was sleep for a week.

'Rustling. Wales.'

Munroe looked up at his Super through half-closed eyes with barely concealed contempt.

Glover ignored the look of disdain. 'There's been another one. It's big money, John. They want someone from the Midlands end. I thought I'd ask you.' He said it as if he was doing Munroe a favour.

'Thanks,' said the Inspector laconically. He wanted to lie down on the slatted bench in front of the battered, grey metal lockers and sleep.

'Well?'

'Why me?'

The DS shrugged his shoulders and turned away, hands thrust deep into his pockets. 'It's up for grabs. I don't want to send anybody too stupid though. Got a reputation to maintain. Thought I'd ask you first.'

Before Glover got to the wire-glazed door Munroe found

the energy to ask, 'Where is it? Wales is a big place.'

Glover came back, took from the inside pocket of his jacket a letter and sat on the bench beside Munroe. He pointed at the word. 'I can't even bloody well say it!'

The two grown men stared at the Montgomeryshire Police document and, with their risible Birmingham accents, tried to make the jumble of l's and t's and s's sound like something. Even Munroe managed a wan smile.

Glover got to his feet. 'Get your head down, John. You're knackered.'

When the Superintendent reached the door, Munroe looked up. 'When do you need to know?'

'Soon. They've had two recently, and they reckon they've got a big one coming off in the next couple of weeks. Get some sleep and let me know tomorrow.' He was half way through the door.

'Any extras, allowances?' said Munroe.

'Wellies,' said Glover, 'standard issue.' And he let the door close behind him.

A young constable with greasy hair and dandruff drove the Inspector through the Saturday morning traffic to the Victorian terraced house in Coleraine Road, Handsworth. At No. 29 the curtains were still closed.

Munroe let himself in and pushed off his still-laced shoes. He climbed the stairs to the bathroom and took a long, unwholesome-looking wee.

As he passed the mirror he glanced at the tired face there. He was thirty-six and looked ten years older. His brown eyes were deep in their sockets and there was an unhealthy mauve shadow underneath them. His nose was out of shape where it had been broken going up for a ball in the penalty area a dozen years ago when he'd been a passable centre-forward.

His mouth was rank with the taste of tobacco and coffee.

He looked like some tired old dead-beat hippy who had smoked too much dope and just come out into the light. And him a cop. He smiled mirthlessly.

In their bedroom he pulled off his clothes and fell into the faintly warm, unmade bed. He pulled the sheets around him and, within a couple of minutes, was fast asleep.

When he woke, it was to the sound of distant laughter in the house. There was a soft light through the curtains at the window and he felt the pang of regret that a sick child feels at having missed most of the day.

From the pavement outside came the sound of a little girl's voice: 'One potato, two potato, three potato, four; five potato, six potato, seven potato, more.' And, with each beat, the rhythmic thrip of the skipping-rope as it tapped the ground.

He opened his arms wide and felt the luxury of the bed and the gift of the deep, solid sleep. From downstairs in the kitchen, and echoing up the dark, quarry-tiled hall, came the far away laughter again.

The kitchen door opened and footsteps slapped on the tiles and then, light and quick, came up the steep stairs. The bathroom door closed noisily and, a few minutes later, there was the muffled flush.

More quietly now, Kath was coming along the landing towards him. She opened the door a crack and peered round. 'Are you all right? I've been up twice. You were out cold.' It was a 'routine inquiry'. There was no affection in it.

She looked pretty. She always looked together in her clothes. Everything about her 'fitted'. She didn't seem to spend any time on it and was rather dismissive of 'fashion'; he'd never seen a woman's magazine around the house, ever. She had small features: good hips, not much waist, a nice bottom, and a shapely little bosom that he never saw but wanted to touch.

Her straight, dark hair was cut to her neck and she always wore a fringe. He rarely saw her forehead, they joked about it. Or had done, once. Her eyes were brown and often looked rather mournful, but it was her mouth that betrayed her emotions: hurt, her lips pursed and lost all of their colour; angry or moved, her lower lip trembled.

She had changed hardly at all in the nine years that they had been married. He was still very fond of her, probably still loved her. But he wasn't *in* love with her any more. Nor she with him, he felt sure. They both knew it and, because they had been in love, they were embarrassed for what had been and was no more. Also, they were both sexually attractive people. Certainly, he still wanted her, almost always.

'I'm OK.' He smiled unconvincingly. 'Could do with a bit of help here.' He looked down at the sheets which were lifting slightly.

'Margaret's here,' she said, as if that explained everything.

He knew it was a hopeless case but tried a futile, 'Give her a cup of tea. I won't keep you long!'

'I can't,' she said, her tone almost convincing him that it was genuine regret.

'Your loss,' he offered feebly as she pulled the door to behind her.

After twenty minutes he got up and bathed. He was rested, but had no energy, drive or motivation. He walked around the pile of clothes on the floor that he had stepped out of, and stared at the jeans and corduroy trousers hanging over the towel rail on 'his' side of the bed. He couldn't make a decision about which to wear, and put his towelling bathrobe back on over clean white underpants.

He didn't want to see Margaret or Kath. He went to the

quiet front room, sat where the last of the evening sun came, and smoked. Snatches of staff-room gossip filtered down the hall: the secretary battle-axe who protected the exercise books from the pillaging staff; the geography teacher's favourite chair in the corner; the unruly kids and their sexual antics in the old block; Chuffer Jones's foul-smelling pipe; the PE teachers' affairs and apparently obligatory sadism.

The distant talk and laughter made him feel isolated and melancholy. He got up and pushed the door to.

He took from the shelf his selection of Philip Larkin and sat there with it in his lap, unopened. The smoke from his Gold Leaf wreathed slowly towards the ceiling. As a lorry rumbled down the quiet street he felt the glazed front door shudder in its jamb.

There came a protracted, almost hysterical laugh from the two women in the kitchen. And then a glass smashed to the floor. After a long moment's silence the laughter rang out again. He looked at the pencil sketch of the balding middle-aged, poet-librarian on the cover of the book. The laughter rose again from down the hall.

He went to the bookshelves in the alcove, reached down the atlas, and looked up Llantrisillio in the index.

CHAPTER FOUR

Sometimes Hopkins waited for the girl until nearly half past nine. He worked around the sheds and barn, tinkered with this and that, piled things here and stashed them there, but all with his eyes flicking back and forth to the cottage door a field away, watching for any sign of movement.

One morning it rained cold sleet and, as he stood there, a hessian sack around his shoulders for warmth, his nose running, she came out in a man's long coat, filled a bucket with water from the tap and hurried back indoors. It is what she must have done for the first few weeks of their stay, before the early April sun had changed her habits. He wanted to shout to her: 'I've been here an hour, forget the cold and rain, it'll make no difference, you're going to get wet anyway.' But he only mooched off testily to his work elsewhere on the farm.

Another day she was there before him. It was a fine morning and as he came round the side of the shed she was already drying herself. So now he came early and, on those mornings that she kept him waiting, stayed late.

The man washed too. He was a dark-haired, spindly youth with no belly yet and wiry arms. And his hair was worn like a woman's; long, far too long, and sometimes it was tied at the back. He, too, washed his private parts at the cold tap, but Ieuwan walked away then. He had no interest in him.

Ieuwan might have made it his business to introduce himself to the London couple. He could have seen to it that he went by on his aged Massey Ferguson as they walked up to the place where they parked their old Bedford near the well. Or, when they were in the garden, he could have been at the bottom of the field, just across the stream, and they would have had to talk. But because he watched her every day, he did none of these things.

Humphreys-the-post brought more information: their names (two different ones); the postmarks on their envelopes (London, Birmingham, Gloucester, 'abroad'); and the paper that they read on Saturdays (the *Guardian*), and gave it to all the interested parties in the area. He became something of a celebrity. He was invited in to farms and cottages that he had never seen inside before. He made his information last, rolled his words, took his time, drank the tea down before committing himself. People went along with it. Talk this good was rare. The man was fêted. Let him have his day. This time would pass. Bill Humphreys would be on the doorstep again and glad of the shelter of the porch soon enough. But for now, let him have his day.

On the evening of the tenth day of watching her, Hopkins answered a knock at the kitchen door and there the couple stood. His ruddy face flushed scarlet. He knew they had come to confront him.

'Who is it, Ieuwan?' called his wife from behind him in the kitchen.

The farmer stood before them, his fingers tightening on the handle of the door in the dark porch, and was mute.

The young man, fearing that there was something wrong with the farmer, and also a little afraid of his silent stare, called back into the space from where the woman's voice had come, 'It's James. James and Susie from Well Cottage.'

She bustled past her husband said, 'Come in. Come in, dear.' And to Ieuwan, in the same breath, 'What are you doing there, man, let them come in.'

He followed them into the low-ceilinged kitchen and the couple stood there awkwardly beside the humming Rayburn.

'Some tea,' said Glenys warmly and, with both her hands, lifted the big kettle on to the hotplate.

Across the kitchen, the farmer's eyes kept darting back to the woman's easy bosom while his wife made the necessary talk to the young couple.

The woman answered, the young man nodded in agreement. He looked a bit younger than her. Ieuwan resented him. It was him that she washed from between her legs each morning.

The farmer's wife spoke slowly in front of the visitors. It was strange for Ieuwan to hear her using the foreign language in their own kitchen.

And she was telling them everything. They were bringing things out of her. But she couldn't see it. He would have held back. Glenys was too trusting. Who *were* these people? What were they doing here? Not the business that they were talking to her about: London, noise and traffic and smoke and no air. Everybody lived like that in the towns, but they didn't come here and find places. And where were their people? Glenys couldn't tell them enough. She worked in the local shop and knew the village talk. But *these* people were from outside. She was giving everything away. And for what? Hold back, he thought.

But she was off again. Now they were laughing. The boy as well. And he smoked, rolled Golden Virginia and then folded the packet down very carefully and slowly. Ieuwan lit a Woodbine from his packet of ten. The girl took the tobacco from the boy's knee and rolled a cigarette too. She was deft. He had never seen a woman roll a cigarette before. She took the matches from the boy's hand without a word, without stopping listening to Glenys who was telling her about the fish van that came to the village on Fridays and the travelling public library that stopped outside the school once a fortnight.

Ieuwan didn't trust them: they must know more than

this, from London. The woman laughed and drew herself back. Ieuwan pretended to laugh so that he could watch her. But when he looked up he thought that the boy had seen him.

They wanted to know if the boy could get work 'anywhere around here'. A day or two to start, and then see how it went. He was getting the dole. It wouldn't be sensible to give it up straight away.

Glenys wouldn't speak for Ieuwan on this. Hopkins enjoyed the power. This was better. This was how it should be done. They were asking for a job.

'You want to do some work?' he said disingenuously, and carefully rolled the ash from his Woodbine into the glass ashtray. 'But you're not going to tell the dole office?'

'Just for a while,' said James. 'Until we see how things work out.' He was embarrassed by what he thought was the man's gormlessness.

Hopkins was enjoying it. But he couldn't go on. Glenys knew his guile, and she would scold him. When he had stretched the moment until it would break, he said, 'You don't want to do a day or two with me? I could find a bit. I wouldn't be able to pay a lot, of course,' and, before the boy could answer, 'Of course, you wouldn't want a lot, with the dole and all, eh?'

James started work the next morning. Three weeks ago he had been driving a lorry around busy London streets. The evenings had been spent with friends in Camden and Notting Hill listening to music and smoking cannabis. Now, here he was, striding up the hill to Ty-Uchaf, going to work for a Welsh sheep farmer.

From his vantage-point behind the barn Ieuwan saw the youth approach. The boy's job had obviously led to changes in the domestic arrangements at Well Cottage: the erstwhile naked woman had not been glimpsed this morning.

Just as the young man climbed over the fence at the top of the field, rocking the flimsy post as he did so, Ieuwan saw the girl step out of the cottage door and stretch herself in the fine morning. He greeted the boy with a terse rebuke about not climbing fences that didn't have stiles or gates, it broke the posts, then the sheep got out, then he had to spend all day looking for them. James, a little surprised by the man's crustiness, mumbled an apology.

The farmer led away from the sheds and barns and into the farmyard so that the long-haired man would not see his own woman washing naked at the tap.

When he had bump-started the tractor down a little incline, he braked hard and James imagined he was to jump on, but he could not see where. Ieuwan, sitting on his metal bum-shaped seat, on a folded sack that he had carried with him, indicated the swinging metal frame at the back of the throbbing vehicle. James stepped up and the tractor lurched away with a jerk, wrenching James's arms at the sockets as he clung to the big, flared mudguards.

They joined the lane that went towards the village and then forked left and climbed towards a field that lay on a slope just below the tree-line. As they got to the field gate, Hopkins stopped and waited, looking at the five bars of rusty metal. There was an awkward pause until James realized what was required. He jumped down and struggled with the hook, which had to have the weight of the gate lifted from it before it would budge, and then unwound a complex loop of baling twine. As he drew the gate open Hopkins drove through without a sideways glance.

They were to cut thistles. Hopkins explained that if you cut them now, just as they appeared, they didn't grow, and then they didn't seed, and you thus prevented future labour.

The scythes were in the corner of the field under a tarpaulin with some other bits and pieces: twine, wire, drums of chemicals and stones for sharpening the blades. Ieuwan began. James watched. Hopkins said nothing. The farmer had an easy rhythm. He approached the renegade plant, swung smoothly through it and severed it near the ground.

James set off on the awkward gradient. He found the tool unwieldy and nearly sliced into his shin within the first five minutes. When he did hit the weed, he hit it several inches from the ground, leaving an untidy stump. Sometimes he hit the plant at the wrong angle, and the blade itself made little contact, simply pushing the sinewy plant over without breaking it.

After an hour that seemed like half a long day he was heartily fed up with walking at an uncomfortable angle across a thistle-laden field with a silent companion in the distance. His size eleven feet ached as he tried to keep his lanky frame upright on the sloping ground.

After another half an hour the farmer called him over to the parked tractor. From a canvas bag he produced a vacuum flask and they shared some lukewarm milky tea. James drank from the grubby, plastic inner cup.

The farmer took a Woodbine and lit it. James rolled a cigarette. But by the time he was ready to light it, the farmer was ambling off towards his scythe again. 'See you at dinner-time,' he said over his shoulder as James got to his feet and arched his aching back.

When he jumped down from the tractor outside the cottage that evening, Susie came to the gate to greet him. They always read the country column in the *Guardian* on Saturdays. But *real* farming! She couldn't wait to hear.

He lay at forty-five degrees in the armchair and turned up the palms of his hands. The blisters that had formed by tea time in the morning had broken by dinner (which Mrs Hopkins had put on the table as they walked through the kitchen door of Ty Uchaf at twelve o'clock) and continued to ooze sharp pain and thin blood throughout the interminable afternoon.

By two o'clock there were no new positions in which he could hold the smooth wooden handle of the tool. He had already taken the jaunty handkerchief from around his neck and pressed it into service on the worst of the blisters, but the relief that it had afforded was only momentary.

As the afternoon ground on, James became convinced that the farmer was involved in some sort of mental battle with him, and he, too, became engaged in an imaginary and increasingly hostile dialogue with the rocking figure who worked a hundred yards away.

These imagined exchanges galvanized him: he resolved to suffer his pain and not to show any weakness.

He carried on, stopping only occasionally to crouch on his haunches and roll a cigarette and, at about three, with an uncanny silence between the two men, to drink another cup of the dreadful weak tea that had never tasted so good.

As he lay in the chair, Susie called excitedly from the back room where the Calor gas stove stood, 'What was it like, then? Come on, do tell.'

He mumbled back, 'It's not like the bloody Ladybird books, that's for sure.'

By the time she brought the Nescafé, he was fast asleep in front of the little fire.

CHAPTER FIVE

The nationwide foot and mouth epidemic that broke out in the autumn of 1967 had put an abrupt end to all rustling for over six months, but things were, at last, returning to normal: Welsh spring lamb was at a premium in the butchers' and all the recent restrictions on stock movement and the attendant fears of infection were over. For rustlers, it was a good time to go back to work.

Running sheep and cattle was a curiosity. It was sporadic. It was seasonal. But the trade was always worth a few grand and it didn't involve confronting security guards or bank clerks who often appeared to be inordinately enthusiastic about dying for their employers, just as long as the tabloid press gave them a front page headline the following morning.

But 'the sheep-shaggers', as everyone from Detective-Superintendent Glover down to the greenest PC on the operation resolutely continued to call the rustlers, seemed unable to make up their minds. The Superintendent's talk of something coming off 'in the next couple of weeks' proved groundless, and Inspector Munroe repeatedly went up and down from Birmingham, through Wolverhampton and across to Welshpool headquarters as things looked promising, and then returned as they went stone cold again.

The initial word that something was on had come from Ronnie Cotton, an armed robber who was due up at the Central Criminal Court in Birmingham during the next few weeks. It was expected that his visit to the court in Steelhouse Lane one day in June would be his last appearance in public for a very long time. He was less than sanguine about the prospect of a long stretch and was prepared to trade anything he'd got to ensure that he might see his young children again before they had forgotten who he was.

While on remand in Winson Green, he had heard on the underworld grapevine a whisper about a rustling blag that was due to come off soon. To the Birmingham CID, he milked it for all it was worth. And it was worth a bit. He gave them all the information he had: a key name or two, a Birmingham address and, crucially, the name of the actual village in Wales where the heist was to take place. It was good information, and it might reduce his eventual sentence by three to five years. His own future would remain uncertain, though. These things always got out. He would doubtless have some anxious shower-times and sleepless nights in Long Larten or Winson Green.

And now it was wait.

One of the villains, John McInnerey, a weasely Scotsman with a mock-Tudor house in Sutton Coldfield, owned, apart from his fruit-machine and juke-box franchising company, one of Birmingham's licensed abattoirs. If and when the load arrived, it was surely he that was going to dispose of it.

Munroe was co-ordinating the Midlands end, and had even managed to get a brawny cop taken on at McInnerey's abattoir in Bordesley Green. His counterpart, Detective-Inspector Tony Rees, and his team was ready in Mid-Wales.

Rees had narrowed the choice of likely targets around the village: one afternoon, in the incident room at Welshpool police station, he had patiently explained to Munroe that you couldn't drive a ten-ton cattle truck up to just anywhere around here (even in the middle of the night, *especially* in the middle of the night!) and have half a dozen thugs load it up with reluctant, noisy sheep. Hardly anything moved in the countryside without local people noticed.

On the other hand, if the villains went too remote, there would be difficulties of access and gathering: upland farmers always spent a day driving their sheep down from the hills before penning them in somewhere and loading them up the next day for market. Rustlers wouldn't have the luxury of that much time.

Munroe, whose knowledge of the countryside was limited to a twice-yearly drive to the Lickey Hills on the outskirts of Birmingham, nodded sagely.

The Welshman explained to his colleague that local knowledge and 'reconnaissance' (his careful enunciation of the word concealed the fact that what it had meant in reality was himself and his sergeant poring over their local ordnance survey map) revealed only two or three places in Llantrisillio where there were flocks grazing, that had lanes wide enough for a big stock truck, and that were not overlooked by some house or cottage or farm. Each of these locations was staked out.

It was no good alerting the landowners: this was a small community and the word would be all around the area within a day. And, if that didn't warn off the blaggers, the farmer would probably organize a bunch of twelve-bore vigilantes who would pepper the next hapless tourist who happened to come by with a caravan and a Birmingham accent.

No. The police decided that they'd keep their operations to themselves. And so, for over a week now, as soon as there was any suggestion of movement at the Midlands end, the Welsh teams dug in at dusk and stayed there through the night. It was cold and April wet. And they were getting jerked off with it.

The Welsh boys soon began to resent the Brummies, thought they were being made fools of, became convinced the information must be duff. In Birmingham, the policemen who sat by telephones and tape-recorders and lay bent double in cars and vans for hours at a time, wished that they had stuck to banks and jewel thieves.

And then word came. It was definitely on. The phones between the main players in Birmingham were buzzing. Some of the messages were engagingly, naïvely cryptic, but in the usual, absurd way.

Munroe was no cryptologist, couldn't always finish the *Daily Telegraph* crossword, but even he could decipher a tapped telephone message that went, 'What sort of load are we expecting?'

'Twelve hundred feet,' came the leaden answer.

Munroe was touched. Although, tantalizingly, they refused to name the farm, he phoned Rees immediately and said that the thieves were aiming to steal about three hundred sheep. They were due to leave Birmingham at seven the next evening.

In the third-floor operations room in Colmore Row in Birmingham city centre, and over at Welshpool headquarters, the mood was jubilant. They were on.

CHAPTER SIX

Early the next evening, a white Vauxhall Cresta was trailed from McInnery's house in Sutton Coldfield to the abattoir in Bordesley Green. Here, three more men joined it. They drove out of Birmingham, through Wednesbury and up to Wolverhampton, the fat tyres hugging the tarmac under their weight.

In the back streets of Wolverhampton, the Vauxhall turned abruptly into a haulage contractor's yard in a run-down part of the town near to the canal.

Ten minutes later, a Thames Trader stock wagon made its way out of the big gates and rattled along the rutted streets on to the main road.

Munroe, in his Zephyr Six, overtook the lorry as he sped towards his rendezvous with Inspector Rees at Welshpool HQ.

It was mid-evening when the truck stopped at a roadside pub in Nesscliff, outside Shrewsbury. A minute later, four policemen in a fawn Hillman Minx drew into the car park and parked in a quiet corner.

A mile up the road, just outside the village of Knockin, an unmarked Rover waited in a lay-by.

Just before closing time, and in a warm, thin drizzle, three members of the gang climbed up in to the cabin of the truck; two others continued their journey among the straw in the back.

In Llantrisillio, twelve miles to the west, three groups of wet, nervous policemen, kept informed of developments by short-wave radio, sat among the dripping trees and bracken.

The plan, such as it was, necessitated the surrounding lanes being blocked (once the sheep had been loaded), the waiting pool of police reinforcements being called up by radio, and the rustlers being apprehended in possession of the stolen animals.

It was a good plan. And it would work. In theory. In practice things never went according to plan: radios didn't work; someone was taking a piss when he should have been taking a message; vehicles broke down and ran off the road; people took wrong turnings and got lost; criminals changed their minds at the last moment; information was awry.

Four of the policemen, Sergeant Gareth Perry and three constables, were dug in in the beech copse on Rookery Hill. Plas Trisillio Hall was half a mile away, the woody smoke from its chimneys wafting towards them.

Another group of four was on the side of steep Pentrefelin.

On the other side of the river, looking down to the village from the bristling furze of Mynydd Glas, sat a third knot of burly policemen, huddled so close together that, as the rain petered out, they could smell the damp warmth of one another. They watched as car headlights on the main road appeared in and out of the hedgerow trees before winding away from the valley bottom up to lonely farms, or on to the next village.

At ten forty-five the few cars on the Horseshoe Inn car park began to leave and, twenty minutes later, Cyril Liptrot plunged the pub into darkness as he went up to bed. The few remaining lights in the village went out until, by twelve o'clock, only the schoolteacher's was left on. Then he, too, retired.

They identified a smallholding here and a cottage there, the last, faintly illuminated landmarks spread out in the darkness before them. They watched as downstairs lights went off, upstairs ones came briefly on, and then another building disappeared from the valley sides.

Seen from Rookery Hill, in the midnight drizzle, Plas Trisillio Hall had lost its hard, stone edges and softened into an indistinct grey mass which hovered below Perry and his soaking men in the cloudy night.

On Pentrefelin, above Well Cottage, James and Susie's nanny goat bleated to the night air. The cops lying there giggled, but it was laughter in church: it covered their real fear.

The men on Mynydd Glas watched as a set of headlights came slowly along the main road and then turned into the lane beyond the village.

On Rookery Hill there was a quickening of the collective pulse as the lights approached them. Between the squally gusts of wind they could hear the drone of the engine as it laboured up the steep lane.

It rounded the last bend, stopped beside the five-bar gate of Geraint Morris's field below them, and the diesel engine shuddered to a halt.

Sergeant Perry buried his head in his cape, switched on his pencil torch and turned on the radio receiver. It crackled, and he winced. He whispered a hoarse instruction, 'Rookery. Rookery. It's here. All units. It's Rookery. Get into position. Over.'

There was the dull buzz of the frequency signal. He moved the dial a fraction in his cold fingers and there was a response. It was a familiar voice uttering a familiar incantation: '. . . *Channel Light Vessel Automatic: rising seven, falling, more slowly . . .*' 'Fucking police radios,' he said.

And then nothing. They waited. An interminable, eerie silence. The huge stock truck below them, waiting menacingly in the gloom; the policemen, aware of one another's shallow breathing, lying prone in the wet grass above.

A shrieking owl made them start. A whole hour passed with only the sound of the wind in the trees and the creak of their waterproofs as the men moved a limb for respite.

At one o'clock, the doors opened. They could hear the muffled voices of the men fifty yards below. And then the sprung truck door was lowered on to the lane. The field gate was unlatched and several shadowy figures darted into the field, their blurred silhouettes skirting the hedges.

The bleating grew as the flock was herded towards the gate, the grey huddle moving down the slope under the agitated guidance of the accompanying shapes. The gate swung open again and the mass funnelled through. The noise of the sheep on the wooden ramp, deadened by sacks spread on it, was reduced to a brisk thunder of drumming hooves.

As soon as the rear door was banged shut, the engine throbbed into life and, on sidelights alone, the lorry pulled away.

Before it had disappeared round the bend, Perry and his men stumbled down the wet grass and bounded over the fence on to the lane. Jeffries slipped headlong on the sheep droppings that lay everywhere; the others, not quite sure what the plan was, or whether there was any plan at all, loped after the vehicle on foot.

At the T-junction before the river, the truck turned left and the driver notched it up into a low-revving third. They were doing twenty-five miles an hour and following the line of the undulating hedge along the lane.

Round a bend, there was an outline shape fifty yards ahead. Suddenly, from the shape, four powerful headlight beams dazzled him. He braked hard and came to a juddering halt. There was a cacophony of bleating and tumbling hooves as the ewes hurtled forward.

The driver sat transfixed, but the passenger door opened and a man leapt from it and ran back down the lane. At the bend he was met by Perry's chasing men and bundled to the ground.

The Birmingham police contingent in the Hillman and the Rover screeched on to the scene and joined the chaos and euphoria among their Welsh colleagues.

The drizzle had almost stopped and there was a warm, surreal quality about the night as Munroe and Rees leaned against Munroe's car and smoked.

At Well Cottage, Susie was awake. Some little squeak or bleat or squeal of the country night had woken her.

She moved her hand up James's leg and laid it over him.

He had never been so exhausted. All his nerves and sinews and limbs had ached with unfamiliar tiredness. All he had wanted, needed to do, when the weariness had abated enough for him to relax, was to sleep.

She sidled up the bed and put her breast to his lips. He sucked. She wrapped her fingers lightly around him beneath the sheets. He murmured his acquiescence as the vessels swelled with blood and filled her hand. When he was big, she eased him into her.

He feigned sleep; she enjoyed his drowsy compliance.

Her breathing became shallow and rapid and her thrusts on to him fast. He relinquished his pretence of sleep, put his hands around her buttocks and pulled her down on to him.

Suddenly, in the night, there was a distant, unfamiliar crash. She stopped, arrested, drew back from him. He had heard nothing. He pushed against her. She waited. A second. He was half out of her. Silence. Another tantalizing moment, he pushed up again. She listened, heard nothing more, let herself down on to him in an ecstasy of delayed pleasure.

At Plas Trisillio, Dorothea Somerville came to the lattice window of her bedroom. There were car headlight beams skewed across the bottom lane at crazy angles. She opened

the old casement and could hear on the breeze the sound
of distant voices. Through her vodka haze she wondered
what it all meant.

CHAPTER SEVEN

In 1968, at the Chelsea School of Art, Charlie Somerville was your man. By the time of his second year at the School, the handsome boy, louche and easy-going, was supplying a wide network of his friends, and they, in turn, their friends, with Afghan and Moroccan hashish, methedrine for all-night partying, cocaine for stints of work, and LSD for the more foolhardy adventurous.

This was drugs for handsome people, nothing sordid and baleful; these were youngsters with wealthy parents, and brothers and sisters who went out with pop stars; brothers and sisters who *were* pop stars.

From the age of sixteen, at his minor public school in Shropshire, Charles had regularly smoked a little dope. All his friends did. And when Michael Laing, a year older than Charlie, went up to Oxford, Laing had introduced him to his dealer in London, and from that time on, it was Charles who ran the discreet little business at the school.

When he got to London, in 1967, the whole world seemed to be turning on. He actually had to restrict the number of people he was supplying, the business threatened to overwhelm him. And although the underground press suggested a change in the law was both inevitable and imminent (Timothy Leary going so far as to suggest that as well as dope being legalized, there would soon be deer grazing on Charing Cross Road), the authorities, as yet, did not share the emancipated attitude of Charlie and his many customers to the aromatic herb, *Cannabis sativa*.

Charlie himself no longer smoked that much hash, for while he knew that The Doors and Frank Zappa and Captain Beefheart did a lot more for him stoned than straight,

its use definitely did not assist him when it came to what
had, in recent years, become his over-riding obsession:
horse-racing.

As a boy, he had been around bloodstock, and grooming
and riding had been an integral part of his life, but gradu-
ally, since arriving in London, the dormant gambling gene
in him had grown with the unpredictability of a malignant
cell.

And now, at twenty, he *was* a gambler and, in a sense,
he was an addicted gambler. But he was not—and here
was the crucial difference—he was not a compulsive gambler. He *could* leave a whole day's racing alone. But, when
the moment was right—the race, the jockey, the handicap,
the odds and the ground—he plunged. And he was doing
very well.

His knowledge of horses and form was altogether greater
than his knowledge of art. He knew a bit about the history
of painting, could tell a Tintoretto from a Titian, spent
the occasional afternoon in the Tate or the National, and
sometimes wandered into a smart gallery on Bond Street.
He had even found himself in the Prado a year or two ago
while changing planes in Madrid on the way back from a
stay with relatives in West Africa.

As far as his own ability was concerned, while he had
some technical competence, he had little feel or touch and,
more importantly, he knew that, as a painter, there was
nothing that he really had to 'say'. But the fact that he was
never going to make any kind of waves as a painter did not
concern Charlie in the least. He didn't mind one jot.

During that first year at Chelsea, he had the sense of
being in exactly the right place at exactly the right time.
He had a lovely photography-student girlfriend, Rachel,
whose father was something in the City; he got up late, spent
the morning poring over the *Sporting Life* and form guides,
spent the afternoon listening to the racing commentaries in

gloriously seedy betting shops. And in the evening he ate out and partied late, often going to bed at dawn.

And the excesses of this happy lifestyle were provided, not courtesy of a father who, while he had land and property, frequently didn't have a red cent in his pocket nor any black on his bank statement from one year's end to the next. No, the cash that kept Charlie in Chelsea clover came on account of the requests for half an ounce of red Lebanese here, a few tabs of acid there and, the icing on this particularly delicious cake, a decent win every few days on the horses. For Charlie, making money really was like falling off a log.

And all this time, this happy time, was just time out: within the next few years, maybe five or seven, or ten at the outside, Charles would himself be administering the family estate of several hundred acres of Montgomeryshire, supervising the management of the dozen tenant farms on its land, and planting oak and beech for his son eventually to copse and his great-great-grandson to fell. There was a natural order in things, and Charlie's relaxed and confident manner came as a result of his knowing that he had an exact place in that order.

Things were about to change.

A friend of a friend wanted a big deal. A really big deal. Charlie checked out with his friend, someone on the fringes of the music business, that the buyer was kosher. He was all right. He was the lighting man with an up-coming band. There was no problem with him. His regular source had run into a problem with the law and he was looking for a new supplier. He was selling on to the people he was working with, members of the band, the roadies and the crew. They were going to be on the road for seven or eight weeks, and trying to score could be difficult in the middle of Nottingham or Hull when you didn't know the scene there.

The deal was set up. It was mostly hash, and a bit of acid. And it was a lot: not a £50 fine, but a long prison sentence. The hash alone was the size of a housebrick.

Charlie couldn't carry the cost himself. His supplier, a dealer for a criminal 'family' who had moved over into drugs three or four years ago, told his boss that Charlie needed credit for twenty-four hours. Charlie was a regular, a boy with a bit of class, a decent flat in Chelsea. The deal and the short term credit, strictly twenty-four hours, was OK'd.

On Thursday evening, as Charlie waited outside Mornington Crescent tube station, a dark blue Mercedes saloon pulled up. Charlie approached the car, the rear window glided down and a small blue holdall was passed to him. Nothing was said and the car slipped away into the evening traffic.

The next morning Charlie saw Rachel approaching the art college and dodged the traffic to reach her on the other side of the road. When he had spoken to her on the phone the previous night he had told her things had gone wrong, but said he could say no more. Now he had her by the elbow and was marching them down Manresa Road.

'What is it, Charlie? Charlie, you're hurting my arm. Can we walk a bit slower?' She pulled her elbow from his grasp and they slowed down.

'Sorry,' he apologized.

'It's OK. What happened, then?'

'Let's have a coffee.' He looked over his shoulder again and they went into the Italian coffee shop off Carlyle Square. A pretty Italian boy brought them Cappucino.

'I was robbed. It was a set-up. They just took the gear from me. There was nothing I could do. No drama. Nothing. Just very scary. The one guy had a shooter. I thought they were going to top me there and then.'

'Oh, Charlie, why didn't you say on the phone? I would have come round straight away, you know I would . . .'

'I didn't want you involved. I don't now.' He slurped the milky coffee bubbles.

'But if they've got the hash, what are you afraid of, they won't hurt you?'

He wanted to hit her. It was a reasonable question and she didn't know how the deal was set up, but he was so afraid he wanted to knock her off her chair. He stayed calm. 'I owe for the gear. I had it on credit. It's got to be paid for today. These guys, they don't mess around. They gave me a day. A day they mean. They'll want their money.' His lips were moving but his teeth were together, he was spitting the words and clenching his fist beneath the smoked glass table.

She lit a cigarette. There was a long silence between them. She felt sorry for him but was sensitive to his anger at her. It didn't help.

She composed herself and risked another question, 'What happened? When you took the stuff? Was it an address you'd got?'

'I took it to the address in Camden that Andrew, fucking delightful, "Oh yes, the guy's all right" Andrew, gave me. It didn't feel right, not exactly. But what does? Down the steps to a basement, knock at the door, a guy comes and in I go. Next thing two big bruisers are standing there, one behind me, one blocking the way to the kitchen. And without a word the one gets out a dull little-barrelled gun. Just points it at my chest from three feet away. It's not like in the movies, believe me. I would have given them my grandmother just to get out, let alone a holdall full of dope. The guy said, "No cops," and then, "As if you would," and grinned. I put the bag on the floor and walked.'

'Whose flat was it, then?'

'The bloke sitting there, I suppose. He wasn't part of it.

He looked out of his mind. Syringe and a stash of horse on the table. Maybe he was Andrew's "kosher" mate. Maybe he'd been set up. I don't fucking well know.'

He rarely swore and it sounded strange to her. She reached beneath the table and took his hand in hers. 'It'll be all right, Charlie, honestly. We'll work something out.'

He squeezed her fingers, but his hands were clammy and he let her go. He wanted her to know how afraid he was, but he wanted to *tell* her, not for her to see him quivering.

'I've got about a hundred and fifty,' she said. 'It's so near the end of term. My allowance is nearly all gone. But you can have that, of course.'

'Thanks,' he said. 'I've got about six hundred in the bank, I'll get that. Can you get yours soon. Bring it to college, in an hour, say?'

'Yes, of course. But what are you going to do?'

'When you've brought the money, stay away. Keep away from me. Stay away from the flat, stay at your own place. I'll contact you when I've got things sorted out, OK?'

'OK,' she said, reluctantly. 'But what are you going to do?'

He leaned across the table and kissed her quickly on the lips, 'Folkestone,' he said.

She looked puzzled, her flecked, blue eyes full of concern for him, 'Folkestone? The ferry?'

'No. The race course.'

Even as Charlie was being robbed, he had had to acknowledge the painful fact that there was very little that he could do. If you were operating outside the law, your only protection, ultimately, was that you had the required muscle to enforce the conditions of your business arrangements. The man with the long, straight nose, wide nostrils and pistol in his hand had seen that Charlie had no way of enforcing his conditions. He was trading on goodwill. And that April

evening in a basement flat off Camden Square, the man
had decided to foreclose on that capricious quality.

As soon as Charlie had got back to his flat he had phoned
Andrew. Andrew was mortified. How could his contact, a
mate, do this? It was a disgrace. It wasn't in the spirit of
the thing. He'd never have anything to do with him again.

That was fine, said Charlie, 'But what about my money?
How am I going to get it back? I owe two thousand pounds
to some very difficult people. They don't do things our
way.'

There was a hint of desperation in his voice that Andrew
had never heard before, and didn't much like. 'You've got
me,' said Andrew. 'I just don't know,' and he hung up.

Charlie had paced the flat and phoned a couple of close
friends. There was sympathy and the offer of a bit of cash
and, from each of them, just a suggestion of their enjoying
the drama: real hoods, and a shooter, indeed. And did
Charlie also detect a hint of *Schadenfreude*? Charlie, who
always had it so good, had taken a little fall. Nothing ter-
minal. He'd walk again. But there was a cloud passing in
front of the sun that always seemed to shine on the boy
from the Welsh border country.

Maybe they were entitled to a tiny gloat.

At noon, Charlie called at Lloyds in Old Church Street
and withdrew the five hundred and ninety pounds that he
had on deposit there. With the hundred and fifty that
Rachel brought to the refectory at lunchtime he had a substantial stake.

In Coral's, off the King's Road, he sat in the corner on
one of the high stools and stared at the *Sporting Life* that
was pinned to the wall. There was a huge disparity between
actual race courses and the High Street bookmakers that
lived on the body of the 'sport'.

All that Jockey Club veneer of decorum at Epsom; the

urbane voice on the public address system at Fontwell Park;
the bowlers and umbrellas, champagne and sandwiches in
the marquees at Royal Ascot; the Jaguars and Mercedes
in the car parks; the women tottering on their high heels
into the giving grass, their knees incongruous in the open
spaces and fresh air.

Charlie had stood at the rail at Sandown and heard the
thundering hooves beat the hard ground, heard the jockeys
swearing at each other and themselves and their mounts.
He'd heard the horses' rasping chests and seen their
haunted eyes as they flew past. He knew the smell and the
sound and the true fear and excitement.

And here he sat, in the corner of the room, as the punters
trailed to the window and pushed betting slips and folded
notes through the little hatch to the shirt-sleeved man on
the other side.

Even the petty, two-bit Pinkies that Charlie despised,
and who lived outside the Silver Ring at Brighton, the clerks
and couples, out for the day with their pound each-way,
backing horses that shared the name of a favourite nephew,
at least they were in some *relationship* to what was happening, there and then on that day, and in that place.

But *here*? The King's Road? This crowded, smoke-filled
room? Formerly, he had always enjoyed these afternoons.
He had been detached. A take it or leave it observer. But
now, he, too, suspected that his frown betrayed the look of
quiet desperation that many of the other punters wore.

He started on the two o'clock at gloomy Folkestone and
had a result, but the price was a paltry two to one on.

He backed his next, safe, short-odds choice heavily, only
to hear it beaten by a head by an eight to one outsider.

Charlie was now in the spiral that he knew was lethal to
any percentage gambler. He was chasing money on horses
he didn't want to back. His best judgement told him that
they were not the ones he should be on, but the pressing

need to pay his creditor sent him to the betting-shop window with yet another wedge of blue notes.

He had the six to four winner in the three o'clock. But then lost virtually all that he had accrued on the three-thirty.

Around the corner from the bookmakers he telephoned William Hill and wagered up to his credit limit of two hundred pounds on the second favourite in the handi-cap hurdle for two-year-olds, the uninspiringly named Maureen's Date.

After an agonizing wait back in the betting shop the result was announced. In a photo-finish, his horse was declared the winner at seven to two. Of the two thousand pounds that he needed, he still had only, on paper, nearly seven hundred.

He phoned through the seven hundred pounds that he was now in credit on his account and staked it at eleven to eight on the favourite, Bridego Bridge, in the next race.

He would still be a couple of hundred short, but he'd got a bit in the building society down the road for a rainy day. And it was certainly drizzling. He'd use that to top up his debt.

He returned to the bookmakers and stood amongst the litter and cigarette ends as the race commentator described his horse making the early running in the two-mile chase. It was clearing hurdles that the trailing horses crashed through. With three to jump, it was several lengths ahead. There was a stumble at the second last. Maybe a foolish punter had made a sudden move at the fence. There was always a knot of people gathered at the fences on country courses, perhaps hoping gruesomely for a fall, perhaps just thrilled by the excitement of horses flying through the air and then smashing through the hurdles at thirty miles an hour.

The second-placed horse began to make the running. At

the last fence, the two horses breasted the birch-twig fence together, but Bridego Bridge had lost its stride and rhythm and ploughed through the hurdles, crashing to the ground. The excited voice on the Tannoy described the fall of the favourite and then followed the winner's progress over the line.

The little group that had gathered near the fallen horse saw it twitch once and then convulse as its nervous system shuddered out of life.

The bruised jockey, a pathetic figure in his bright colours, cradled the huge, vein-swollen head in his hands. The horse's imploring eyes rolled. Only thirty seconds after hitting the ground, it was dead.

Charlie was still alive, but very pale on his stool.

CHAPTER EIGHT

Mickey Gynn was surprised when Charlie didn't turn up with the cash the following evening at Mornington Crescent tube station.

Gynn had graduated from being a small-time Walthamstow crook to a dependable messenger and enforcer for his employers, the Maitland family.

The Maitlands had used him several times, on bank cheque frauds and credit card scams, and found him up to the work. He didn't stick out a mile while standing at the counter in some Old Street bank. He could pass for a businessman, perhaps not someone entirely legitimate, like an insurance broker or shipping agent, but something marginal, perhaps a minor record company executive or someone doing well out of the rag trade boom.

The first thing that Ken Maitland had done was give him his nickname. Stood at the bar of the Duke of Wellington in Leyton, the old-style East End boss had said, 'Give Mr Gynn a Gordon's, Frank.'

The little entourage laughed at the feeble joke and Mickey, from that day on, had had the awkward and confusing handle of 'Gordon's'.

Now, he sat in the front passenger seat of the Mercedes with his hands clasped behind his head and his legs stretched out before him. He felt affronted.

Ibrahim, the blue-black Senegalese who drove Mickey when they were at work, sat hunched over the big cream wheel of the Mercedes 190.

At ten past eight Mickey drew himself up in his seat and said to his silent companion, 'Well, well, we've been stood up, mate. We'll wait a bit longer, but he won't come now.

We'd better give him half an hour, so we can tell the boss. But I'm telling you, he won't come.'

Ibrahim switched on the tape-player, pushed his broad shoulders back into the soft leather and reclined the seat. The two men sat impassively as Dusty Springfield went through a medley of her hits.

Two minutes after the arrival of each tube train way down beneath them, a gaggle of people emerged in front of the yellow-tiled station. But there was no Charlie.

Ibrahim turned the tape over. Half way through 'You Don't Have To Say You Love Me', Ibrahim's particular favourite, Mickey said, 'Let's go and check his drum, I'm pissed off sitting around here.'

As they pulled away from the kerb, Gynn opened the glove compartment and pulled out Nicholson's *London Streetfinder*. The book opened at Brondesbury Park. He took out the Stanley-knife blade that nestled in the spine there, and dropped it carefully into his jacket handkerchief pocket.

They parked outside the three-storey house in Elm Park Road, Chelsea, and Gynn ambled up the steps and rang the bell. As he waited at the door, he looked down to the Mercedes and watched Ibrahim's lips moving to the words of 'I Just Don't Know What To Do With Myself'.

He wondered how he had ended up working with the only West African in the universe to be tone deaf and totally devoid of any sense of rhythm.

A young woman eventually opened the front door and Mickey uttered a peremptory, 'Charlie,' as he brushed past her and took the wide stairs two at a time up to the first-floor flat.

He slipped a credit card into the Yale lock and the door sprang open. It was a nice, spacious flat. The heavy, maroon, full-length curtains at the street window had been left open. In the sitting-room there was not much furniture, but it was all good stuff: a nice drop-leaf table with barley twist legs; a chest of walnut drawers with a Grundig TV incongruously sat on top of it; a Victorian desk and captain's chair; a big, comfy, floral-covered sofa. In front of the window was a wide trestle-table covered in books and papers. On the floor, the Bang and Olufsen stereo was still switched on. Beside it, in the alcove, was a line of LPs, perhaps a hundred of them.

Through the door on the right was a fitted kitchen. There was some scummy washing up in the sink and an open pot of Marmite on the table; the butter had melted in its greaseproof packet in the radiator warmth of the flat. The coffee-maker had been left switched on and stewed the coffee. Gynn turned it off at the socket.

He opened a wall cupboard, pulled out the Corn Flakes and pushed around tins of tomatoes and beans and peaches. He slapped the pasta in its long blue packet into the palm of his hand and left it on top of the breadboard.

He went back into the sitting-room and through into the bedroom. It was in semi-darkness, the curtains closed. He switched on the light and sniffed at the faint whiff of someone else's bedding and socks. There were some clothes on the floor, a paisley shirt pulled off inside the cashmere jumper that had been worn on top of it, a pair of pants, and a pair of socks in balls that he kicked away from him.

On the bedside table was a book about the nude in history, with an ashtray on top of it, half-filled with stubs. He picked up a fat one. It was the end of a joint, made from the thin rolled cardboard of a yellow Job cigarette-paper packet. He dropped it back into the ashtray.

Inside the drawer of the bedside table was a small piece of hashish, cigarette papers, tweezers, some apricot body lotion, a packet of contraceptives and some loose change.

The wardrobe door was hanging open and he pushed the clothes around. Next to a traditional Harris tweed was a

blue, big lapel velveteen jacket. He checked the label on
the solitary dark suit: it was a Chester Barrie. Mickey
sniffed the expensive cloth, fingered the fine, hand-stitching
on the lapels and smoothed the back of his hand down the
cool lining.

Back in the sitting-room he sat and mooched around at
the trestle-table that was covered with art work and books.
He looked with a kind of askance fascination at a big book
of Otto Dix. He tired of the grotesquerie and pushed it
aside and drew to him the next big book.

He carefully turned the pages of Edward Hopper's work.
He preferred these; the people were recognizable. Some of
them looked like crooks, or at least people with secrets; and
there were lonely, sad women who might be whores. These
people had stories to tell. He found himself quite interested
in what the man at the hotel window might be doing there.

He walked to the window. Ibrahim was drumming his
fingers on the steering wheel.

On the floor by the settee was yesterday's London *Evening
Standard*. There was also something called *International
Times*, with a picture of a child on the cover smoking a
joint, and a garish magazine in pink and green called *Oz*.
He'd seen it on the news stands. It looked unreadable.

He went to the roll-top desk and looked for an address
book or letters, but there were only bills and receipts: for
brushes, paper, books and framing material. There were
theatre ticket stubs and a dry-cleaning counterfoil and a
bank statement from Lloyds. This time last week Charlie
was over four hundred pounds in credit.

From the shelves in the sitting-room he pulled down
books at random. They were mostly paperbacks. Some he
knew: Ian Fleming and Len Deighton and Dennis Wheat-
ley. Others he'd seen on the station bookstalls: *Catch 22*;
Portnoy's Complaint. Some he'd never heard of: *Catcher in the*

Rye; *Island*; *Brave New World*; *Nineteen Eighty Four* and *Animal Farm*.

Amongst the hardbacks, he fanned aimlessly through a Charles Dickens, and then a Thomas Hardy. Pasted into the flyleaf of *The Mayor of Casterbridge* was a label: *Presented to Charles Somerville, Third Year English Essay Prize, Oswestry School 1962*. He slipped the book into his jacket pocket and left the room.

Downstairs in the hall were individual letter-boxes made of metal grille. There were two letters in the box marked Charles Somerville. It was unlocked and he reached in and took them. When he turned, the girl from the ground-floor flat who had let him in was standing at her open door watching him. He didn't look like anyone that she knew, and he certainly didn't look like one of Charlie's friends.

She was about to speak, raise some sort of objection to his presence in their hall, when he waved the letters at her. 'For Charlie. I'll let him have them. I'm going to be seeing him. 'Bye.' And he pulled the heavy door to after him.

CHAPTER NINE

It was a late frost and James had not wanted to get out of the bed that he had built for them along the wall of the main room of the cottage. They had kept the little fire in all night, and it was pleasant snuggled up together, naked and warm.

He put his fingers down to her and they made love in a sleepy, relaxed, early morning way. For another ten minutes they lay on their backs, side by side, fingers entwined, and then she rolled away and put sticks on the fire and the saucepan on to the Calor gas stove for coffee.

He washed at the tap, the cold air about him, the pale sun on his shoulders, and smelled her on him. But for his work at the farm, he would have gone back to her again.

He drank his Nescafé, ate a slice of toast and tied the laces of his new work-boots with double bows to the same length.

As a hippy, James would have made a very good insurance agent. Even though he looked the part, with his shoulder-length hair and jumbo-cords, he had never really achieved the relaxed persona that was *de rigueur* in 1968.

When he had met Susie at a party in Kensal Green, he was ripe for some sort, any sort, of conversion. They listened to The Beatles, made love, went on anti-Vietnam war and CND demonstrations, attended the Buddhist temple at East Sheen on Sunday afternoons, read Krishnamurti and chanted their mantras in the top-floor flat off Cromwell Road.

James had no difficulty in convincing himself that folding his shirts neatly (which he had always done) and chewing his pasta mindfully (they had only ever had spaghetti from a Heinz tin in Birmingham) was the same thing as being a Buddhist.

For James, this time in London was growing time. But he was never wholly at ease there with their drug-oriented friends. He wore the 'Legalize Cannabis' badge the same as everyone else but, in a secret ballot, his paper might have been, at the least, spoiled.

The temple and the chanting was OK. And their friends *were* friends. And the job driving a lorry was all right, and Susie said that maybe he should enrol at a college in September and do some GCEs. But then a friend at Susie's work, a secretary at St Mary's Hospital in Paddington where she was temping, told them about her home village in the Welsh hills.

It sounded unbelievable: empty cottages, space, a village pub. Why not make a break? Not the familiar Eastern trail that half their friends had done: Kabul to Katmandu and, finally, Goa before, six months later, ending up back in Notting Hill.

What they were contemplating was a real move. A move for life. James liked the sound of the arch phrase. Susie laughed and said it sounded like a building society advert. But she was just as keen. There was a new excitement in their lives. They'd do it. They'd up sticks and go.

They made phone calls, wrote letters, handed in notice, said goodbye to friends, bought maps and an old van to carry their possessions, and went. It was the best thing they'd ever done.

Boot laces neatly tied, jeans tucked into ex-army woollen socks, James got into the old Bedford. This morning, in convoy with Hopkins's stock truck, they were going to move sheep up to the higher ground.

The old van started in spite of the cold and he drew off

up the lane towards the farm a mile away. But the trickle from the stream that skirted the hedge had spilled over on to the tarmac and left a sheen that the tyres could not grip.

The sun had started to thaw the land. The frost on the slates at Well Cottage was trickling down into the gutters.

Susie stood naked in the doorway and felt the glow of the sun on her body. She closed her eyes, drew the chill air into her nostrils until there was a little ache, and counted her many blessings.

She could hear the Bedford sliding on the lane and James revving it too hard. She smiled.

Hopkins, concealed beside his barn a field away, had never seen her so completely, and for so long.

After half a dozen times, with the clutch burning and the van snaking about the narrow lane, James gave up, engaged reverse and backed down to their parking place. He would go the longer way round, down to the bottom road that led to the village and then up through the long, gentle climb to the rear entrance.

The move to the country had rejuvenated their relationship: in London they had often talked of parting. Now they were getting on well again, better than ever. Alone, together, they shared everything. There was no dilution. They talked, walked together, sawed wood at the horse that he had made, split logs with the big axe that they had bought with great pride at the agricultural merchants in Llanfrynach. And they made love. At least every day, often two or three times.

They saw things that they had forgotten since primary school. Watched birds building, saw badger setts, discovered the flowers and trees coming into bud and leaf as if this was the first time that any of these things had happened. And, in a way, it was.

She turned to the tap and started to wash. The farmer

unbuttoned himself as she began her familiar movements. He accompanied her, his rhythm following hers. He would not wait too long, but too soon would be to waste her.

At Pentre farm James turned off the ignition and rumbled down the back, little-used track. The chained Border Collies knew his sounds and smell and ignored his coming. There was smoke from the kitchen chimney, but all was quiet.

He walked to the slatted, wooden barn and looked across the hill. All down the field opposite him the sun was drawing back the white line of frost and revealing, each moment, more and more of the green grass to its touch.

The smoke from the chimney at Well Cottage rose straight up in the still morning. Susie was at the tap. He was shocked and yet charmed to see her there. He felt a little resentment at her nakedness which mixed with the vicarious pleasure of seeing his woman, unobserved.

The fences and trees had started to steam in the warmth. She remained there, naked, her back to him. He watched, mesmerized.

There was a human sound a few feet away from him. It was wrong. He walked to the corner of the barn. As he rounded it, the farmer, standing in the shadows, panted and shuddered.

James advanced on him. Hopkins straightened up and pushed himself into his rough trousers. But no words came from his mouth. He looked quickly from the wiry boy to the girl a field away, and back, but no sounds would come.

CHAPTER TEN

Cyril Liptrot's first thought was that the man must be lost. But the tall black man standing bowed beneath the ancient timbers simply smiled at the publican and asked for a rum and Coke. Liptrot folded his *Daily Express* and poured the drink in silence.

At that moment Ibrahim's companion strode into the bar with a breezy, ''Morning. Lovely day.'

'Yes, very nice,' replied the publican. 'What can I get you?'

'Bottle of Guinness, please,' said Gynn.

Maitland had told them to wait for a day or two.

They played snooker, had a bet, collected rents, visited the pimps and hookers working their patches, and moved some dope. And several times a day they sat in their car outside Charlie's flat, and watched. There were callers. Youngsters looking for a five-pound deal or to borrow a record, they guessed. The girl downstairs answered the front door to them, and then they left.

One of the letters that Gynn had taken from the mail-box was a chummy missive from Charlie's younger sister, Louise. It was written on headed notepaper. The place shouldn't be hard to find: there couldn't be that many Plas Trisillios in Llantrisillio, Montgomeryshire.

On the third day, Maitland said to them with a weary air, 'You'd better go up to his place and find him. Get the money. The two grand, plus inconvenience and expenses.'

'What if he's not there? He could have gone anywhere?' asked Mickey.

'Look, Gordon's, if he's not there, use this.' He tapped

his big skull. 'Have a word with his mater and pater. Tell them you're collecting a debt. Take a painting or two off the wall. I don't fucking care. Just come back with the dosh. He's making me look a prat.' And then, humorously, but filled with his dangerous rage, 'But take it easy. Keep your heads down. It's not the Smoke. People'll notice you. Especially Mister West Africa here, in Llan . . . Llan . . . wherever it bleeding well is. Go on. Piss off. And don't give credit to bleedin' art students again.'

As the landlord poured the stranger's Guinness, Mickey, hands thrust into his pockets, cold blue eyes fixed on the overweight landlord and his thin lips pursed, defied the man to open the interrogative conversation that he so dearly wished to have.

Ibrahim peered down at the photographs of the village football team which were yellowing on the wall.

The two men took their drinks over to a table beside the cold fireplace, and Liptrot re-opened his newspaper on the oak counter.

They said nothing. The black man stretched out his long legs before him and swirled the rum around the glass. Mickey looked into last night's ashes.

As Liptrot turned the page to Dempster's column, he missed the few words that one of them eventually spoke.

Gynn came to the bar, 'Any sandwiches?' he asked.

'I'll see,' said the landlord and walked to the door marked Private. He took a look back at the men before he disappeared into the back room.

When Mrs Liptrot brought them their food she registered no more surprise at the men's presence than if they had been two of the local dominoes team, 'Would you like mustard with your beef? Or some pickle?' she asked, and walked away to get both without waiting for a reply.

Liptrot had ceased to be surprised by his wife's increas-

ingly quirky behaviour. Only last week he had heard her
say to a bemused regular at the bar, 'Isn't it strange how
the sheep graze the grass to all the same length?'

After they had eaten their sandwiches, Gynn said good
morning to the landlord and the two men left the silent
bar. Liptrot went to the window and watched them climb
into their big car and lumber away past the ancient church.

Mrs Liptrot looked down at the uneaten crusts on
Ibrahim's plate, 'His hair won't curl when he grows up,'
she muttered to herself.

They had no intention of driving up to Plas Trisillio, asking
for Charles Somerville and starting to pull his fingernails
out. But they did need to see him, see what his 'position'
was. Was he out of funds? Was he trying to go criminal?
Or had *he* been blagged? Why exactly had he done a runner?
How was he fixed? There was no point crippling him until
they knew what they were trying to achieve.

They took pot luck and forked right at the hump-backed
bridge over the River Trisillio. A mile up the lane the grazed
and ploughed fields gave way to parkland that was dotted
with mature trees.

Eventually they came to an avenue of beech trees that
lined a drive which disappeared into shrubs and greenery,
only to emerge again in front of a big, sombre house.

As they drove slowly past the gate-house and cattle grid
at the bottom of the drive there was the name, fashioned
into the wrought-iron gates: PLAS TRISILLIO.

CHAPTER ELEVEN

James was a man whose glass was always half empty, never half full. He had never been able to believe his good fortune in having Susie and there was, in his fatalistic mind, a certain inevitability about the fact that one day she would leave him.

The fragile confidence that he had developed, both in himself and in their relationship, had been shattered by the one quaking jolt of witnessing the gross act of the farmer satisfying himself at the sight of her.

His gnawing suspicion that, while she *was* his woman, she would never wholly be his, had been perversely confirmed in this one shocking episode.

At first, when he had returned and told her about Hopkins, although distressed, she had made little of it. But when she saw how hurt he was, she comforted him. It seemed to make him worse.

He attacked her directly, said it was her fault. She fought back. Defended herself against his unjust rage. She had to wash herself, she said. What did he want? *Of course* it had been awkward and unpleasant for him, coming upon the man like that. She understood that, but it was the pathetic farmer's problem, not theirs. Couldn't James see that?

Blinded by jealousy, the abiding image of the panting farmer feeding his paranoia and insecurity, he could not.

In this poisoned atmosphere, and now without his job, the spring days following the incident became long and oppressive. They worked around the cottage and garden, but there was a leaden formality between them.

Confined within the little cottage, the evenings were

worse. The nights, when they finally came, were interminable as they lay stiffly side by side in the narrow bed.

On Saturday evening they went to the Horseshoe to escape the confines of the cottage. She assumed a false jocularity with the labourers at the bar. In fact, her apparent good humour was genuine relief at the temporary escape from his sole, dour proximity. He seethed. Her laugh filled the crowded bar. He could have ground his glass into her face. He drank quickly and far too much and at nine o'clock he lurched to the car park where he was sick. He came back and drank more beer, the taste of vomit still on him.

When she suggested that they go, he bought more drinks, waving a five pound-note at anyone with a glass.

The village football team returned from an away game. They were callow boys, drunk and loud and emboldened by their win and the alcohol.

Liptrot sensed the trouble. James swayed at the bar, slurred his few incomprehensible words and could not focus. His hand gripping the pint glass on the bar, he listened to the easy talk between Susie and two of the footballers behind him. The beer had freed them of the inhibitions that generally made them so polite when they passed in the village or met her in the shop.

Something was said in a lascivious undertone. He crashed his glass on to the bar and turned and struck at the big boy in one frenzied movement, all his anger making him strong and wild. There was screaming as the boy scuffled the long-haired drunk from him and landed sharp blows to his face and shoulders.

She was between them, pulling and yelling and crying. In the yellow light and cigarette smoke, the people watched, fascinated and amazed as the hippy newcomer from Well Cottage, and Ralph Jones from the council houses were pulled apart and stood and snarled and grunted at one another.

On the glowing fire a log shifted, and the murmur of the pub picked up again. A table was righted and people began to leave. The boy's friends stood close about him. Liptrot poured James's beer down the sink and nodded his head towards the door.

Susie stood at James's side as he rocked and throbbed. He held a handkerchief to his nose and tilted his head defiantly back. He tasted the clots of blood as they ran into his throat. Swaying, drunk, hurt and ostracized, he felt better.

The little card stuck in the window of the village Post Office came as a blessed relief.

She banged the green door at the rear entrance of Plas Trisillio. The Colonel answered it. He towered above her, straight-backed and youthful in his faded corduroys, cotton shirt and old Guernsey sweater.

'Hello, I'm Susie. From Well Cottage. I've come about the morning job.'

When he heard the imploring tone in her voice and sensed the surprising urgency in her manner, his stern face softened into a warm smile. She responded with a quick, tense smile, immediately felt awkward, like a schoolgirl, and looked away.

He was charming and polite, even deferential as he walked her slowly through the yard and into the stable block. He asked her what she knew about horses. He knew everything, and here was she, one yellow rosette on top of her wardrobe back at her parents' home in Gloucester, gushing like a child. He walked by her side, his head inclined to her as he listened carefully.

When they reached the stables, she approached a black mare whose head peered out of its stall into the afternoon sunshine. She stroked the mare's mane and blew gently into her gaping nostrils. The horse nuzzled her and snaffled back appreciatively.

Ten minutes later, as she drove down the drive, Somerville tipped his cap to her, and she smiled genuinely.

Back at the moody cottage she tried to cover the yawning gap in their relationship with her enthusiasm for the job. But in their hearts they both knew that she had pounced on the work as a lifeline, an escape.

On the Friday afternoon of the first week of her working there, James insisted that they go to bed. She felt that she was being tested, and reluctantly complied. They had long, cold, uninvolving sex, in which he remained detached, monitoring his mechanical performance, and observing her closely. When he hurt her, she cried out, but he watched her through feelingless eyes, and carried on. Later, he tried to apologize. She made little of it, but she was hurt.

While she was at her work with Somerville's horses, James fixed the fences to keep out Hopkins's ewes, cut wood and dug out the couch grass and elder in the vegetable bed.

When she came back (and he watched the clock and strained to hear the whine of the old Bedford as it started to climb the bottom lane in first gear), she related the news of the morning: the Hall, unsteady Mrs Somerville, the Colonel, their pretty daughter, Louise, the other workers about the estate, the horses, the mare that she had exercised. And he listened to it all carefully. And then he questioned her.

She knew what his fears were, and carefully omitted any friendly words that might have been exchanged, any kindnesses offered, any admiring look that might have come her way, from the grocer's boy to the Colonel himself. She gave him only plain, unembellished fact. The sort of truth that is always untruth.

He saw a bloom on her, there was about her something new. He was convinced that there was something going on at Plas Trisillio. He knew that they were finished. She had left him in all but name.

He had to have her. But she didn't want him. He was urgent.

She said it was her period. But he knew that she had barely started. He knew her cycle as well as he knew the phases of the moon and how they affected *his* behaviour. It was rising now and he was frantic. At this time, his semen was always up. It was no old wives' tale about virility and fertility. Planting crops when the moon was new, nourishing them with water that had stood beneath a moon that was full; these things made them grow well, every country gardener knew this. The staff on the wards of the mental institutions knew that the heavenly body's power was no myth.

But she said no, she said that she had started, had some discomfort. 'Do you mind?' she asked considerately.

Did he mind?

The next afternoon, his pent up fears and insecurity exploded. Out of nothing, a tiny tiff about how to light the fire, he rose to sudden fury and leapt up from the grate and struck her with the back of his open hand. He was as shocked as she was. She was frightened out of the tears that wanted to fall, and didn't cry, just put her hand to her swollen cheek in disbelief.

He rushed out of the cottage, up the slope and through the woods of Pentrefelin. He was gone two hours. When he came back, he apologized again. He was in turmoil, he said, and had no idea why he had hit her.

They sat in front of the fire for a long time in silence.

Her swollen cheek that had partly closed her eye above it was a reproach to him as he stole a look at her.

Eventually she said, haltingly, 'Everything was beautiful . . . and then that thing with Hopkins . . . It is a paradise here, but they're only people.'

He looked at her imploringly.

'I'm so sorry,' he said.

And he was.

CHAPTER TWELVE

Charles was relieved to be home. Very relieved.

He had asked Len Hughes to bring him to the rear entrance of the Hall. He wanted to surprise his family, he said. He watched as Len drove away.

His mother was delighted to see him. He put his arm around her bony shoulders and drew her to him. She was skeletal: frail, striking, brittle. She wore her black hair brushed defiantly back off her high forehead; her sharp features and deep-set eyes had an angular beauty that refused to yield to her innate despair.

She asked him how long he would be staying, but then wandered absent-mindedly out of the kitchen before he had begun to answer her. When she came back in, she stood close to him as he made coffee, and asked him if he would like to have a friend over. 'He could stay for tea, if you like.'

He thanked her. Most of his old friends, he patiently explained, were away. Either in the army or at agricultural college or university.

Louise, home for half-term, was always pleased to see her big, easy-going brother who could charm her girlfriends to distraction, and she hugged him to her.

When his father came in from the estate for lunch Charles told him that he was home for a few days to do some landscape drawing for his portfolio. He fancied the change. There was no problem at the Art College. He had come up on the early Saturday train to Welshpool and taken a taxi from there to the Hall.

Only Sophie, the family's brown and white Jack Russell, behaved out of character: instead of yapping around the boy's ankles, she ignored him, sniffed at the door to the vestibule, whined for some minutes, and was then sick on the kitchen floor.

He was tired and would have a lie-down, he told his parents. He kissed his mother lightly on the forehead. As he pulled the kitchen door to, carrying a wooden tray with coffee and biscuits on it, he heard his father's exasperated voice, 'Can't you leave it alone? It's not even lunch-time yet . . .'

Upstairs, the coffee went cold, the biscuits remained uneaten as, exhausted, Charles fell asleep.

The next morning he ordered by telephone the *Sporting Life* and the *Racing Gazette* from the newsagent in the village. They were to be placed in the clay land-drain pipe that the delivery boy would find at the rear entrance. Charles would settle the bill himself.

On the Monday, he was up early and went straight to the rear gate. The fat racing papers were stuffed into the pipe. He took coffee to his room and spent the next two hours in unbroken concentration trying to decipher the form and breeding of horses which, unravelled correctly, would open the bookmaker's coffers.

He came down to eat some breakfast at ten and then returned to his room where he went over his myriad calculations again. All things being equal, Ribble Valley should pass the winning post before any of the other eleven horses at Wincanton at a little after two forty this Monday afternoon.

His mind preoccupied, he traipsed down the drive heedless of the bunches of pale daffodils and the grey-barked beech trees. Sophie skipped and hopped and yapped at rustling leaves and fallen twigs.

His father was in the distance working on one of the

horse jumps that were scattered about the fields in front of the house.

Last evening, the two men had sat opposite one another in the Colonel's study as the boy asked his father for a loan. He said he needed some cash. For the first time in his life he asked for money. Not school fees to be paid, or the doubtful privilege of living in a big draughty house, but actual five-pound notes. He knew he was clutching at less than a straw.

Somerville felt perfectly well-disposed towards his children, but in a detached, rather distant way. His children were a part of the warp and weft of his life; they were a thread, but there were other threads in that cloth: there was an estate to administer, horses to tend, trials to organize, hounds to supervise and, of course, his mistress in the next valley to see.

The Somervilles lived apart now: under one roof, they lived separate lives. They rarely conversed. They had their own bedrooms, used different bathrooms. He sat in his study; she watched television in the small sitting-room until the broadcasts ended. There was drink concealed everywhere. But the handsome crystal decanters were no longer used. The bottles came in the back door from the local grocer's van, and she carried them straight to one of her rooms where she slopped the whisky and vodka into big, rarely washed tumblers.

The children no longer knew whether their mother was drinking to escape her wretched state, or whether her plight had come about because of the drinking. They had no idea. They had not been at home to see the marriage fall apart.

His father had listened to him carefully. Charles felt as if he was back in the headmaster's study.

He asked Charles what exactly he wanted the money for.

The boy said it was a 'business opportunity'. It was cast-iron and very short-term. A week, two at the most. He felt his throat constricting. He was aware that the timbre of his voice was hopelessly at odds with what he was trying to assert. He had meant to be strong and now he felt like a twelve-year-old. He was afraid of the Londoners hurting him, doing him serious injury, yet he was too embarrassed to share this simple truth with his father.

The phrases that the boy used were wholly alien to the man. He virtually flinched as the boy uttered: 'business opportunity'; 'cast-iron'; 'short-term'. But he heard him out, and only shifted his long legs once. Finally, his father asked him how much he needed.

'About fifteen hundred,' said Charles.

'Pounds?' said the Colonel.

'Of course pounds,' said Charles, unable to disguise his irritation.

'It's out of the question, of course. I could raise a hundred or two in cash. But fifteen hundred! You'd be better off asking one of the lads on the estate. That's where the money is these days.'

As Charles got to the gate-house, a two-tone Bedford van clattered over the cattle grid and careered up the drive. He stood aside as it shook past. It was driven by a girl in blue jeans, who gave him a smile and wave. He raised a hand as she passed.

CHAPTER THIRTEEN

Sophie sniffed her way along the scented hedgerow as Charles wandered up the lane. They went past the bluebell copse on the corner with its silver birch trees, their white bark peeling, lime green leaves just emerging. At the top of the little incline, they paused and Charles looked down to the back of the Hall. In the distance he could see the fair-haired girl and his father standing together in the stable yard.

There was the sound of a car coming up the slope, its languorous engine throb amplified by the narrow lane and high hedges. He clambered up on to the verge and called the dog to him. Sophie trotted around his feet, out of the path of the approaching vehicle. As it neared them, he reached down to hold the dog by its collar, but the car accelerated and lurched up the grassy verge across him.

He was trapped against the hedge. The passenger door of the car sprang open, and he was pushed further into the sharp, leafless thorns. A black man was on him and at his throat, his hands clamped around his neck. The engine of the car throbbed, and the dog circled the man and barked frantically.

The man released his grip, but as soon as Charles lifted his hands to his neck, he felt a crippling blow as Gynn's iron fist sank into his stomach.

He folded with the sickening pain and collapsed to the ground. The dog was demented. Gynn swung his pointed shoe at the little bitch and kicked it away from him. There followed immediately a pathetic whelping from where the dog lay broken on its side.

Charles covered his head and looked out from watering

eyes as the men stood above him. The birch trees behind them moved slightly in the breeze.

The man he knew only as Mickey appeared to be taking in the landscape. He didn't look down at Charles as he said quietly, without emotion, 'You owe us money. You've put us to a lot of trouble.'

Charles didn't want them to talk about how much trouble they had been put to. He was certain that it would correlate with his own intense suffering. He tried to interrupt and gagged, backing as far into the roots of the hedge as he could, 'I'm getting it. I'm getting it. That's why I'm here. I'm trying to get it together.' He pushed the small of his back into the hard spiky roots of the blackthorn.

The man didn't respond. He didn't seem to have heard. Charles's bowels were hot. The man took something from his top pocket. The sharp, bevelled metal glinted between his thumb and forefinger. He still looked over the hedge into the middle distance, taking in anything and nothing, focusing nowhere. He took a deep nasal breath, as if about to begin something unavoidable but regrettable. The voice was still devoid of feeling. 'We don't do credit. It's a strictly cash operation we do. I gave you a day, by arrangement. You didn't pay. Worse, you went away. We've had to come and find you. It's all time. And money. My boss doesn't like it. He thinks we're on holiday up here.' The dog started to skulk away, a cry with every step.

Charles had no place to go. His voice was quavering, 'I just need a day or two. Honestly. I had a problem. The guy who wanted the stuff. They turned me over. But your money's coming, honestly. That's why I'm here.'

Gynn looked down to the high chimneys of Plas Trisillio. He was derisive, 'You've got all that, and you want me to wait for a miserable couple of grand? You've got plenty. I want mine.'

There was a frightening finality about his words.

Charles started to cry. 'I can't get it just like that. I need another day, maybe two, that's all. I swear, please.'

As Gynn bent down towards him Charles instinctively covered his face. For a moment he felt nothing and then there was a searing ache and his calf was hot and wet and blazing with a terrible, rending pain. The shock cauterized his tears and mobilized his instinct to survive. He was terrified that they were going to kill him, but his jaw set and his look conveyed only loathing and defiance, not the pain and fear that convulsed him.

Logic should have told him that they wanted their money, and anyway, wouldn't kill him on a country lane outside his own house. But they had followed him this far. They had cut his leg, long and deep. They were not normal people. They could do anything.

Gynn moved his foot, and Charles took his sticky, blood-soaked hand from his calf and tried to shield his head. But this time the man just drew his black shoe slowly through the damp grass to remove the mud that marked it. Charles lay there, the wet grass on his lips, the pungent earth in his nostrils, all of his senses startlingly alive.

'You've got today and tomorrow. This time Wednesday. Right here. And *don't* go away. You'd find out what we *can* do. Not only to you. You've got people down there.' He nodded in the direction of the Hall, 'A little sister.' He looked at his watch. 'Wednesday. Half eleven. Here. No mistakes.'

Charles watched the car sink on its springs as each man got in. A jet of white exhaust smoke hung in the grass as it pulled away and left him wet and crying, relief mixed with the pain.

CHAPTER FOURTEEN

Charles wrapped his handkerchief tightly around his leg and limped across the lane and up the little bank into the birch copse. Out of sight, he tried to clean his hands and leg with damp leaves and grass.

When the bleeding eventually stopped, he lifted the handkerchief from his calf and looked at the gash that the blade had sliced open. His stomach heaved as he saw how deep the incision was. He propped himself up against a tree and lit a cigarette. The nicotine made him giddy but the blue smoke was a familiar comfort.

The dog whimpered up to him, lay by his side and whined. After he had cigarette-burned through the double stitched and hemmed part of his shirt, he was able to tear off a strip all the way round below the waist. He made a better bandage from this, one that wrapped twice around the wound and could still be tied.

An hour later, having wrestled a stake from a newly pleached hedge nearby, he limped along the lane. He tried to disguise the pain at the same time as not putting weight down on to his injured leg. Frequently, the blood began to trickle down him again, but eventually he crept, unseen, through the stable-yard and up the deserted back stairs.

In his room he put a damp cloth around his neck to reduce the swelling, and bandaged his leg properly with strips cut carefully from an old school shirt.

He smoked another cigarette, cleared his throat and tested his voice and, when he could delay no longer, he controlled his breathing sufficiently to telephone the bookmakers from the phone on the landing.

*

It was a long wait. He lay on his bed, the terrier at his side, and then hobbled to his bedroom window and watched as his father pottered about with the horse jumps at the far end of the top field, the old green David Brown tractor pumping out its exhaust smoke beside him.

He was on the phone to the turf accountants before the race had finished. The start had been delayed by a few minutes when a horse unseated its rider. He waited and pressed the phone close to his ear to try and hear the commentary on the closing stages.

There were only muffled noises in the background in the office and the incomprehensible urgency of the commentary as the race reached its climax. And then it stopped. He waited. There was the sound of someone at the desk picking up the phone through papers on it. 'Ribble Valley. Nine to four.' There was a pause. 'Hello. Are you there?'

'Thank you,' said Charles. 'Thank you.'

Back in his room, he fell prostrate on to his bed. A great feeling of relief suffused him. He had been right. The favourite, Time to Turn, could not win. The weight was too great. A mile and a quarter, maybe; even a mile and a half with the ground uncharacteristically firm, but not over a mile and six furlongs. The three-year-old simply didn't have the stamina. Nine to four wasn't a great price, and he had not been the only gambler to have unlocked the secret of her potential, but bookmakers were the most cautious men on earth. That's why they came to work in Jaguars while the punters parked bicycles against the wall outside the betting shops.

He lay on the bed and smoked, his arm trailing over the side; Sophie crept over and licked his fingers. At first tentatively and then with feeling. The dog was tasting the blood. Charles managed a wan smile. They were regaining their ground.

*

Charles avoided his father all evening. He called to his mother that he was working and would have a sandwich later. Walking to the lavatory at the end of the passage, he came face to face with his sister. They were both embarrassed. She was clutching something white in her hand. She looked flushed. He took the initiative, played the older brother, and she responded, blurting out an explanation in a shorthand that they both understood, 'Father . . . he *would* come to the barn then . . . I was with Peter.' She unclenched her fingers and a little cotton brassiere unravelled from her hand.

Charles smiled at her indulgently, leaned forward and drew a wisp of hay from her auburn hair, 'Naughty girl,' he said kindly, and then, more seriously, 'Be careful.'

'Of course,' she said, glad of his concern for her, a concern without censoriousness.

She sensed the strange awkwardness of his standing there and looked up at his swollen neck. 'What's happened to *you*, Charles?'

'Oh, you wouldn't believe me. I walked into a branch. I was walking and reading something. I went straight into this branch.' He made a decapitating gesture across his throat and raised his eyebrows in a ham theatrical manner.

'Oh yes?' she said. He was right, she didn't believe him.

His leg was beginning to throb again. But he couldn't move without betraying himself. She smiled at him, came close and planted a little kiss on his cheek. She smelled sweet. 'Night-night,' she said, and turned into her room.

He had frightful dreams that replayed the reality of the day. When he woke it was still black night and the sheet was coiled about him. He struggled free and lay there panting.

The wind was buffeting the house and howling and moaning in the tall chimneys around him. A metal bucket went crashing over the brick floor of the stableyard, and then he heard a slate dislodge from the roof above him and rumble and scrape down the eaves before smashing to the ground.

He leaned on the window-sill and sucked hard on his cigarette. His leg ached. He wished that the light of the morning would come, but there was no sign of the dawn, just the tops of the trees moving in the wind and the rain thrashing at the house.

When he woke at seven, it was to bright sun and showers of fine, gusty rain. The world was fresh and clean and this was its last rinse. From his bedroom window he could see a rainbow that came from behind the house and reached down into the next valley.

At the bottom field, which always drained badly, there was a broad lake of rainwater that had not been there on the previous evening. And beyond that, on the lane itself, there was a fallen ash.

The ash was a curious specimen. Its black buds felt like moleskin to the touch; of all the English hedgerow trees, it was the last to come into leaf, and then, after its brief season, it shed its big, sad, yellowing leaves before any of the other trees. Its grey ribbed bark had none of the gnarled, fairy-tale mystery of the oak, the smooth eeriness of the beech with its almost human limbs. And, to cap it all, this curious, most English tree, would suddenly shed an apparently healthy bough for no obvious reason.

He slipped out quietly and collected his newspapers from the clay pipe at the rear entrance. The muddy drive was running bright little rivulets as the hill behind the house drained its storm water down the fields and into the streams that fed the River Trisillio a mile away.

He took coffee to his room and for the next two hours was lost to everything about him as he engrossed himself in that day's form at Market Rasen. He was over a third of the way to his target and had a big credit stake. He needed only one short-odds winner.

By noon he had made his selection. It was the two-year-old Santa Fe. The horse had travelled nearly two hundred miles across country from his stables in Somerset to take part in the major race of the afternoon, the three o'clock Younger's Cup.

His room was stuffy and the air would do him good. He would walk down the drive and on to the lane to exercise his leg. He couldn't hide from his family for ever.

He got out of the house and hobbled and limped and even, with a huge effort, actually convincingly walked a few steps down the drive. After several minutes he heard a car approaching through the rhododendrons. He leaned against a huge beech and opened his fingers against the bark and began to sweat profusely. It was Mr Jones from the village shop making his delivery. The portly, white-coated grocer waved and drove past.

When he got to the lane, council workmen were clearing the limbs of the fallen ash. Chain-saws were screaming and the wood chips pluming into the air. The tree still had all its being in it. Even as they lopped and severed its branches it remained vibrant, seemed to retain its glistening hold on life.

As Charles approached, they throttled the saws down. They were pleased to be involved in this muscular work. It was, for a change, important, even vital work. And, as if to compound their satisfaction, as they revved up the motors on their two-foot-long Stihl and Husqvarna saws, ready to attack the limbs again, one of the men asked Charles rhetorically where the Post Office crew was. They hadn't even arrived yet. It would probably be days before *they* turned up in their yellow vans and restored the telephone lines. Charles walked to the hedge and looked into the sodden field. Between the fallen poles, and brought down by the limbs of the tall, leafy ash, were the lifeless cables.

Back at the Hall, he lifted the black telephone receiver and heard only the disconnected silence. It was nearly two o'clock. How many other lines were out of operation? Was the village telephone-box also out of order? It probably was. It was almost certainly on the same line as theirs.

He would drive to a phone himself, just keep going along the valley road until he got to one that was working.

His father was trying to start the Land-Rover in the yard. The small trailer was attached, full of conifer rails for fencing. Charles stood at the larder window and watched. The old diesel eventually spluttered into life and filled the yard with black smoke.

As soon as he had pulled away up the rear drive Charles picked up some change for the phone and hurried out to his mother's Mini Traveller. As he approached the dusty car he saw that it was listing. The rear tyre was flat. He swore.

Time was getting short. How far would he have to drive, he wondered, to reach a telephone that was working? He approached his father's Rover.

Should he chase after him, try and catch him, and risk an outright refusal, or simply take the car and certainly incur his wrath? Perhaps if he were lucky, he might get back before his father even knew that he had used it. He smiled lightly at his own deception and climbed into the black 105.

He pushed the seat back several notches, pulled out the choke and turned the key. The six-cylinder engine came to life and he backed out of the wooden building and drove slowly down the drive.

*

The bottom lane was strewn with the twigs and small branches that had been torn away in the stormy night. The drainage ditches on either side were running like streams, the streams overflowing into the fields.

The rain continued to fall in short, gusty showers as the sun broke through the cloudbursts. There was another rainbow in the sky ahead of him as he neared the village. The Trisillio was hurtling under the hump-backed bridge, and piling the water-borne debris from upstream at its funnelling buttresses.

He turned on the radio, but it was *The Archers* and he turned it off immediately. At the rectory he passed the rector, his sly-looking black and white Collie loping along beside him. The elderly cleric raised a hand in acknowledgement.

Once out of the village and on the road to Llanfrynach, he switched on the cassette-player. It was the Mozart violin concerto. He pushed back into the seat. He fancied himself in a film: moody weather, empty roads, a big car, his own real drama, and this music.

He was stealing a glimpse of his father, knowing that he must listen to this as he went across to Llandrinio in the next valley to visit his mistress, Nicola Latham. For as long as Charles had been able to remember, his father was always 'out' on Tuesday evenings.

There was a large branch lying across the road on a bend and Charles braked hard to avoid it, the Rover's long bonnet dipping as he did so. It brought him back to the present and he drove more carefully.

It started to drizzle and he switched on the windscreen-wipers. If there was also rain at the Lincolnshire racecourse, it would help him; his choice would prosper in heavy going.

There was a Post Office van and two engineers working outside the green junction box at the side of the road in

Llanfrynach. There was no point stopping and he drove
through the village and joined the main road to Meifod.
There were fewer hedgerow trees and less debris on the
wider road and he picked up speed a little.

He looked down at the Smith's car clock with its green
hands. It was a quarter past two. He had plenty of time.
There would be a phone in Meifod.

The rain stopped abruptly and a bright sun burst
through. There was a fine little swish as he drove through
the shallow puddles on the long straight. There was not
another vehicle on the road and he accelerated up to sixty
miles an hour. The car was flying over the wet tarmac.

There was a shattering explosion and the wind and cold
was booming and battering in at him. The violin concerto
was still playing but he could see nothing. He swung the
steering-wheel from side to side, but there was no response
from the car.

And then, suddenly, with tremendous violence, for
Charles Somerville, everything ceased.

CHAPTER FIFTEEN

Built in 1958, the anodised aluminium and glass police headquarters at Welshpool was a stark reminder of architectural enthusiasm for the then current ideas, no matter how unsuited to their mileu. If anything said '1958', this building did; as you drove past it you almost expected to hear a xylophone combo playing in the background.

Behind the building were the softly rounded Carno Hills but, only ten years ago, a Swansea architect in his wisdom had decreed that this three-storey oblong edifice, with its blue and yellow pre-formed panels, acres of glass and strips of dull steel, should sit at the foot of these bosomy hills and draw attention to him, and it, rather than merge with them.

The local planning committee had needed only one meeting to give overwhelming approval to the project and, after its completion and opening by the High Sheriff of Montgomeryshire, the architect was never again seen.

Munroe drove up to Welshpool early in the afternoon. There was to be an 'end of case' party, traditional at the successful conclusion of any major inquiry. The Inspector was expected there, plus a few others from the Birmingham end, and more than a dozen of the Montgomeryshire team. They'd become matey with some of the lads. They were a good bunch, a bit slow perhaps, a bit plodding, but solid.

At home in Coleraine Road, things between Kath and Munroe had reached an atrophying deadlock. They had agreed to talk and sat in the kitchen with a bottle of Bell's and some of the sweet Woodpecker cider that she liked on the table before them.

Ten years ago she had been at college in Birmingham training to be an English teacher. He was a raw cop on the beat, two years into his basic training and doing A-levels at evening class to try and get out of uniform and into CID.

There was a charming innocence about their polite chat over coffee in the college's refectory that first evening. He found it hard to understand her interest and obvious liking for him rather than her duffel-coated, wispy-bearded student cronies.

They were all going to the Stage Door coffee bar and folk club. There was some shuffling and awkward delay while she got her coat on. He sat there diffidently, wanting her to invite him.

'Why don't you come too?' she finally said. 'Do you like "folk"?'

'Yes, some,' he said, hesitantly. 'But not tonight, I have to work. Thanks, though.' He looked away, embarrassed.

The next week, when the others left for the club, she stayed seated and said she would join them later. The talk was easy between them. He was a cop because he was interested in people. He had wasted his time at school, achieved nothing, got into fights and scrapes and left early. Since then he had done menial jobs until he had decided to join the police.

It was like a second chance to him and he took it with enthusiasm. He wasn't a brute copper, he was a thinking man, he wanted to understand people, fathom their behaviour. He knew that he had to do this to understand their crimes. He was training to be a cop for the same reason that she was training to be a teacher: he wanted to do some good.

He still lived at home with his parents in Great Barr. She shared a flat with a friend in Erdington. They went to the cinema together, saw *On the Waterfront* and *Blackboard Jungle*, and the theatre to see *Antony and Cleopatra*, her favourite Shakespeare. In a pub near the theatre before the performance, she explained to him the essence of the story, told him to listen for certain speeches.

During the play she held his hand, her fingers closing on his as Antony mused to his lover, '*Here is my space. Kingdoms are clay . . .*' He was moved.

When her flatmate went away later that month they spent their first night together. Neither of them was a virgin, but neither had ever spent a night with a person of the opposite sex. It was good.

Within a year they were married, and for several months they continued to grow and share and learn together. They were lovers, but they were companions too.

Kath was a good teacher. It was the early 'sixties and there was opportunity and experiment and unbridled optimism in the air. Educationally, anything seemed possible.

Her heart was in the right place and the kids at school loved her. Even great hulking fifth-form football yobs listened to her long enough to be snared by her enthusiasm for Steinbeck or Sillitoe.

But she reached a stage where she could not let go: another course, another qualification, another promotion. A new school, bigger department, more responsibility, and then more meetings and more sub-committees to put the ideas into practice that she worked so hard at.

And who was he to talk? He was the same. He didn't even seem to have to work at it. His selection came through and he was out of uniform and down to the Italian tailor in Digbeth that all the young guys used. He felt the part, he had arrived. For the first time in his life he felt absolutely comfortable with who he was and what he was doing. He was the part.

The years piled up. Promotion came. Senior officers left, retired, transferred. They were experienced, but they were yesterday's men. They had been in service during the

Second World War. It seemed a lifetime away: it was another world.

And he *was* a good cop. He had a sharp mind. He knew which corners to cut and when to delegate and when to run and when to hide. His instincts served him well. He even stayed on top of his paperwork. His progress wasn't meteoric, but he moved through the ranks quickly, and to achieve it, he worked all the hours God sent.

And Kath? The cinema? The theatre? It was too painful to think of. What had happened? Where had they gone? Where had they come apart?

She was out most evenings: parents' meetings, staff meetings, Departmental functions, the occasional trip to the cinema with a friend from school.

Nowadays, they didn't eat together, rarely went to bed at the same time, found sex awkward. He fell asleep in front of *Match of the Day*, a whisky in one hand, a Gold Leaf burning in the fingers of the other. He didn't like what was happening; he didn't much like Kath and he didn't like himself at all.

They didn't even talk about having children any more. It had slipped down the agenda, lost in his thoughts of corpses in shallow graves, and hers of reading schemes for slow learners.

He said he had started to feel a stranger in his own home. When she *was* there, there were always people in the kitchen, friends of hers. Yes, they were amiable enough. He'd say hello and they'd say hello but then there was that awkward, vacant smiling until he backed out of the room again.

And so they sat estranged in the kitchen that they had once decorated together, the drink between them. She was exasperatingly literal, said that it was *he* who had just been away, not her. By now, half drunk, he confessed that he spent more time at the police club or doing overtime than he needed to just to be out of the house, away from her and the tension that he felt when they were together.

She fought back. The tension in their relationship emanated from him, she said, not her. They each rehearsed their familiar routines, delivered their hollow, set-piece speeches.

But they both knew that the whole thing was half-hearted. It was an end of season game, there was no atmosphere, the crowd had gone, the stadium was empty. They were going through the motions, but they both knew there was nothing to play for any more.

They drank whilst they talked. And the drink was the sole arbiter. They moved from the treacherous shifting sands of their relationship into the safer, neutral ground of work. He told her about the operation in Wales and she seemed genuinely interested. It was a relief to talk of these things.

By eleven o'clock, they had drunk half the Scotch and all of the cider; the kitchen, where she always preferred to sit, was full of cigarette smoke. They were half drunk and her speech was a little slurred. Her eyes revealed her. Their very wariness towards one another added a quiet excitement to the walk up the stairs.

She had behaved sluttishly. The cider and whisky had freed her. He lay on the bed, his mouth set into the absurd, fixed grin that nowadays accompanied imminent sex or the appearance of a camera.

She slipped quickly out of her clothes and climbed naked on to the bed. He caught a whiff of the sweet cider. She straddled up him, further and further, rocking slightly on the sprung mattress.

He realized that he had actually become a little afraid of her.

At his room above the pub in the High Street he had slept and shaved and now he was back at Headquarters, anticipating a night he wasn't looking forward to. Last night's disquieting and inconclusive meeting with Kath had left him feeling uneasy: the last thing he wanted was to get legless on strong beer and warm whisky with a lot of burly cops.

He pulled his Zephyr into a parking place across from the row of six concrete garages. The Chief Superintendent's chocolate on sable Austin Princess was in the end one. There were a couple of CID vehicles adjacent and then a Ford Transit van. Further up was a Triumph Herald, probably stolen somewhere and abandoned up here, with a yellow 'Do not touch' label pasted on to it. And, in the last garage, there was the horribly mangled wreck of what had been a black Rover.

Inside the austere building it was that early, desperate time of the evening; the room too big, brightly lit and sparsely peopled. There were huge, ceiling to floor orange curtains, not yet drawn, at the plate glass windows in the first floor bar, and behind them, out there in the May evening, the last of the day disappeared behind the Carnos that stretched away to the west.

He joined the small group at the bar and ordered a round, even though their glasses were three-quarters full. Inspector Tony Rees was telling a joke, a sure sign that there was very little happening. He listened and grinned vacantly but, as the punch line arrived, he edged closer to the barman and paid so that he wouldn't have to fake his own hollow laugh. In any event, he'd heard it in Birmingham months ago.

An hour later the atmosphere had thickened: the cigarette smoke grown dense, the volume increased and the beer slopped. The curtains had been closed, but where someone had yanked at one of the big drapes, several curtain hooks had been pulled out and the thing hung there forlorn.

At about nine o'clock Chief Superintendent Nicklin rapped the bar with his glass. He began his vote of thanks by explaining that, in the eyes of the public, witness the press reports, they had been involved with something along the lines of an Ealing comedy. Just as poachers were, in the public's collective mind, good-hearted, wily chaps who were engaged in an unequal struggle against rich landlords and spoil-sport gamekeepers, so rustlers were perceived as a bunch of wayward chaps doing no more or less than rounding up a few sheep. The fact that they were real villains, with real form, were often very dangerous and in pursuit of large profits, was not something that the press, from the *Daily Telegraph* to the *News of the World* was interested in. For the press, it was just a good yarn.

'No matter how many trucks go rolling around country lanes at night; how much surveillance is undertaken, how dangerous the chase and arrest, in the final analysis, there's something faintly ridiculous in grown men, good coppers like you, being involved in all this, just for the sake of bleedin'—sorry, *bleatin'*—sheep.'

As far as the misguided public was concerned, he said, even *cattle* wouldn't be so bad: after all, a steak was a steak, was a steak; a cow a big thing. But sheep? A sheep had never been, and never could be, anything but intrinsically absurd.

But, said the Chief, *they* knew better. They had been involved. They had courted the danger; they had made the dawn arrests; they had apprehended the villains, villains who, if they were not here in the hills of Wales (he swept his arm around to indicate the landscape on the other side of the garish curtains) would be holding up banks and security guards instead. No, let no one be in any doubt, they had done a good job. They had done a *great* job. Not a man or woman here, not anyone who had been involved, would find that their career prospects had been anything but considerably enhanced on account of their involvement with this important operation.

He then paid tribute to the successful liaison which had taken place, and the friendships that had been struck up between 'us Welsh boys and our friends from Birmingham'. (Here he did a quite passable impersonation of Sergeant Joey Cleaton's Dudley account.) And that was it. He counselled the two dozen men and three women to celebrate their success this evening and to keep up the good work. There were a few boozy, 'Hear, Hear's' and then, when they were quite certain that the rambling Chief had finished his tribute, the general hubbub picked up again.

The CS was a happy man. His involvement in the case, as befitted his elevated status, had been, apart from signing one or two warrants and being kept informed of progress, nil. And yet every single national newspaper had mentioned him by name in its coverage of the arrests. The *Western Mail* had even done a feature article on rustling in Wales, in which he had been quoted three times. He was a *very* happy man. Retirement was only two years away. He felt that the chances of being able to look over to the fireside of the large retirement bungalow at Harlech, and see on the mantelpiece the coveted CBE, had been greatly increased during the last few weeks. The trial, convictions and sentencing were a formality. The future looked pleasant indeed. He had another whisky and water and then slipped away to his house on the outskirts of the quiet market town to watch *The Untouchables* on TV.

Munroe stood at the window with Tony Rees and Richards, the big, young cop who had been infiltrated into McInnerey's abattoir in Birmingham. The lad was looking very pale. Ten minutes ago he had been giving the two senior men the benefit of his experience in undercover police work. Now, he was going to be sick. Munroe knew it. He hoped

that the youth did too. He certainly didn't want vomit on
his new trousers and clean shoes.

The lad had become very quiet and started to sway.
Munroe took the initiative, 'I'm going down for a breather.
Why don't you come down too, son, you look as if you
could use a bit of air?' The young man offered no resistance.
He was beyond bravado. They walked away together,
Munroe slightly unsteady, the boy stepping across the
swirling carpet with concentrated purpose.

In the front car park the boy walked directly towards the
bushes that had been planted around the building, bushes
that seemed to bear little relationship to the natural, living
world.

Munroe lit a cigarette and wandered round to the back
of the building where he had left his car. He could slip
away now, but it would be rude. He hadn't said good night
to his colleagues, and the youngster who was now retching
in the dusty evergreens had to be taken care of, too.

A yellow light was thrown into the open garages by
sodium lamps hung from big brackets on the wall of the
main building. Munroe went past the Chief's empty garage, the CID cars and the Triumph Herald.

In the end garage was the crashed Rover. A wreck was
a magnet to him. In his twelve years with the police, he
had never even begun to overcome his fascinated revulsion
at motorized death. The jagged inertia before him rep-
resented someone's violent end: smashed glass, wrenched
metal, stained upholstery. He had seen it all during his
years, but he still felt the trauma, the deep wrench of
his guts. He lit a Gold Leaf from the stub of the one in his
fingers. The boy groaned and gasped twenty yards away.
Munroe sucked hard on his cigarette and took a couple of
steps into the shadowy garage.

The workings of the car that man, with his endless in-
genuity, sought to conceal, were exposed. It was like

putting someone on an operating table and opening his
chest. There: that's how it *really* works. Forget the cotton
shirt, the woollen jumper, the nylon tie and leather belt.
This is the bloody, beating heart that really makes you tick.
Cars are pressed and shaped and painted and smoothed,
upholstered and dressed, all their entrails cleverly concealed. But here was the other side: the bag burst, the pieces
fallen out. The brown, dry metal of the underneath; the
oily places; the doors impacted open, polythene linings and
wires and springs, all spilled out.

The front end had suffered the impact; the engine hous-
ing was concertinaed and the engine casing itself had been
forced up from its mountings. The windscreen had been
smashed out. The driver's head? In spite of himself, he
forced open the passenger door and looked for the tell-tale
signs.

In the driver's seat there was glass and a lot of dried
blood. The bleeding had been heavy. Lacerations to the
face; chest injuries, certainly, but actual death must have
been caused by the skull being fractured on the windscreen
at high velocity. It was only conjecture, but he'd seen
enough in the past, read the reports, written them, given
evidence at harrowing inquests.

Always on the floor was the pathetic thing that he knew
would unhinge him: a cardigan, a chocolate wrapper, a
coin, even a road map, something that belonged to the
person, that made them real, gave them a life, a life that
they no longer had. And here it was. He picked it up. A
cassette-tape box. The Mozart Violin Concerto, the
Deutsche Gramophon recording. His eyes flicked up. The
tape was still in the player. It was still pressed home. It
had been on. This was the last thing that the driver had
ever heard. *'Of life dispatch'd, Cut off . . . No reckoning
made . . .'* He muttered the pathetic words of Hamlet's
father. He wanted to take it out. Take it away and play it.

Start it at this very point, where whoever it was who had died on this windscreen had stopped listening.

He leaned against the rough, breeze-block wall and inhaled deeply. Of course he mustn't take the cassette, or anything else. The whole thing would be the subject of investigation. You never touched evidence. It was a cardinal rule. He shouldn't even be in here.

He pushed himself up from the wall and turned to leave. He looked back into the garage and saw the bonnet. It was leaning up against the wall at the far end. In the shadow he hadn't seen it there.

He went in again and, in the semi-darkness of the far end, looked from the bonnet to the car and back again. It was still almost in shape: an expensive English saloon was horribly smashed and distorted, and yet here was its bonnet which, apart from a few dents and scratches, could probably be repaired by the average car enthusiast.

From the bushes the lad called out weakly, 'Inspector? Inspector Munroe, are you going home soon?'

Munroe flicked the stub of his cigarette away and walked towards the youth.

CHAPTER SIXTEEN

The next morning Munroe called at the station to clear what had been his temporary desk. He parked around the back and opened the boot of his car.

Inside the headquarters there was an air of unusual quiet: last night had taken its toll and there was little of the usual noisy banter. Munroe greeted Rees, who was on the phone, and acknowledged the desk sergeant who had never shown the Birmingham man any friendliness and did not appear to have changed his position today.

From the front office Munroe could see the footsteps that young Richards had left in the soft earth of the flowerbeds as he had vomited into the bushes.

He carried two boxes of files to his car and then sauntered the few paces to the corner of the building. He stood in the full, bright sunshine and looked towards the wreck. He turned and walked away, refusing to be drawn.

Inside the station he shook hands with Rees and a couple of the other men. There were promises to see one another again, but they all knew that it was the kind of pact that is made between holidaying families on Mediterranean beaches.

As he went past the front desk, the hostile sergeant muttered, ''Bye, boyyo.'

Munroe depressed the clutch, pushed the column change up into first and turned the key in the ignition. As the engine fired into life he turned it off, got out of the car and slammed the door hard shut. He swore at himself.

Inside the garage he ignored the shell of the car and went directly to where the bonnet stood. He gazed at it for some moments, followed its long, elegant lines with his thoughtful eyes. He stepped forward and drew it to himself in both hands and ran his fingers down the smooth, lipped metal. As he trailed gingerly down its length, proceeding carefully for fear of tearing his skin, the fingers of his right hand touched something soft.

Munroe had arrived at a notion of evil which was almost apocalyptic: massacres in India; tidal waves in the Philippines; a mudslide in a Welsh village; ritual killings in California. His only rationale for these arbitrary slaughters was a vague theory of a malign presence that stalked the globe, smacking an apartment block to the ground with a petulant hand, stirring the ocean to a fury with a finger and, at day's end, pushing a helpless child into a disused mineshaft, its pathetic cries to go unheeded.

In their early courtship, Kath had offered the troubled policeman Gloucester's lines from King Lear as some sort of panacea:

'*As flies to wanton boys are we the Gods; they kill us for their sport.*'

Not a week had passed since without his mouthing them to himself.

It was these same gods that plucked jets from the sky, crushed Saturday afternoon crowds at football matches, put 'guns in the hands of young children', and here, before him now, had certainly snuffed out a life in the wreck of this mangled car.

But, as a policeman, Munroe had learned to ask, Why? Had Shakespeare's wayward divinities *really* had no help from their dark agents on earth? The apartment block sometimes didn't fall down of its own accord, but because the structural engineer had deceived the building contractor, or because a careless architect had pencilled in a line too thin.

*

'You back already?' said the dour sergeant.

Munroe ignored the facile question, and posed his own. Nodding towards the garage, he asked, 'What happened to the Rover?'

Without looking up, the desk sergeant replied, 'Head on. Hit a tree. English boy killed. More money than sense.' And then, facetiously, 'All right?'

'All right,' said Munroe, and walked out of the door again.

He sat in his car and lit a cigarette. It was too soon after the beer and tobacco of last night and it made him feel heady and slightly sick. When he had smoked half of it he bent it roughly into the ashtray and went back into the rear office.

He called Rees aside, 'Who's on the Rover, Tony?'

'I am. Why?' asked the Welshman.

'Have you come up with anything?'

'What do you mean—come up with anything? It's a straightforward. No other vehicle involved. Lost control. Slight bend and a little camber on the wet road. No booze, according to the post-mortem. Happened last week. We're just waiting for the vehicle examination boys from Cardiff to go over it for the inquest.'

'Who died in it?' said Munroe.

'Local lad. Philip Somerville's son, Charlie. The family goes back generations. Why, do you know them?' he jested, 'No Birmingham in that line, I don't think, John!'

The two men stood in the shadows of the garage and examined the car.

'Why's the front end this smashed, and yet the bonnet's virtually intact?' asked Munroe guilelessly.

'The accident report said that the bonnet was in a ditch by the side of the road. It must have got torn off when the car went through the hedge,' replied Rees.

'What if it came off *before* the car started to crash?' said Munroe.

'Why should it?' said Rees.

Munroe opened the palm of his hand.

'What's that?' said Rees.

There was a blob of white rubber gum an inch in diameter in the policeman's palm. Munroe lifted the bonnet from where it stood and manœuvred it into the daylight. Rees came round to see where Munroe pointed. There was a moist spot where, until ten minutes ago, the gum had been wedged.

Over beer and a cheese sandwich back at the White Horse Hotel in the High Street, little more than a pub with a couple of rooms available for guests, Rees and Munroe discussed their next moves.

Rees's experience of crime had been limited to the Montgomeryshire area, and he had never been involved in anything more serious than a missing person inquiry. (The woman was eventually found: she had thrown herself from the Froncysyllte aqueduct in neighbouring Denbighshire, but her body was not found for several days, and even then, it was by a canoeist on the River Dee, not the police.)

Munroe's experience was wider. He had, as a young DI, already led the investigations on two Midlands murder inquiries: one, the killing of an eccentric homosexual by a male prostitute; the other, a woman by her husband and his lover.

Rees was glad to have Munroe along. And Munroe was tacitly relieved to be able to postpone going back to his wife and an uncertain future in Coleraine Road.

It wouldn't be strictly true, but it wouldn't be a mile wide of the truth, when he phoned his Chief at headquarters in Birmingham and said that something had come up on

the sheep blaggers' inquiry which would delay him for a
few days longer.

By the time that they were having their second pint in
the bar of the White Horse, they were having their first
disagreement. Munroe wanted to keep the lid on his suspicions. Experience had taught him two things about interesting or important investigations: if they were interesting
enough, someone higher up took them over; and even if
they didn't, you soon had half the division getting involved
and blocking out the light. There was a world of difference
between having the assistance of people when you wanted
it, on house to house, or forensic, and having every Tom,
Dick and WPC getting in the way of your inquiries.

DI Tony Rees would have none of it. The notion of not
keeping his boss and colleagues informed was anathema to
him. It was dishonest and unprofessional and, he argued,
it would probably prove counter-productive. On a local
case like this, his colleagues on the force might well have
information to hand that he and Munroe could spend days
looking for.

Munroe was touched by his friend's gauche faith in his
colleagues. 'But if something's going on,' said Munroe
patiently, 'if someone interfered with that car, the sooner
they know that there's an inquiry under way, the sooner
they can try and cover their tracks. It's true in Brum, so it's
even more so out here where nobody farts without everyone
knows.'

While Rees resented the disparaging allusion to his close-
knit community, he reluctantly recognized the force of
Munroe's argument. There was a little hiatus as each man
sipped his beer. Rees's pride would not allow him to cede
such an early victory to the other man: it would somehow
undermine his authority as resident cop.

For Munroe's part, the lure of the mystery was overwhelmingly seductive and determined his preparedness to negotiate. At this moment, nothing would have mortified him more than to get into his car and drive back down the A5: there was a mangled wreck in a police garage a few hundred yards away from where they were sitting; a young boy lay dead in the local undertakers, and in Munroe's jacket pocket, in a little piece of polythene, was a blob of rubbery gum. It was out of the question that he should leave now.

Appearing to draw on huge reserves of magnanimity, Munroe said, 'Look, let's split the difference. For a couple of days, three at the very most, let's see what we can turn up. And then, no matter what, we'll go public. What do you say?'

It was a face-saver. The sort of acceptable compromise that diplomats and trade union negotiators spend hours and days behind closed doors trying to arrive at.

Huddled in the corner of the quiet lunch time pub they pooled their thoughts. Rees had seen the place where the car had left the road. It had flown through a hedge and hit an oak tree after sliding thirty yards across a wet, fallow field. There was a slight bend on the road, but nothing much. The road had been damp and a bit greasy. It was the night after the big storm. Munroe had been in Birmingham.

'Could he have killed himself?' asked Munroe disingenuously.

'Well, he did!'

'You know what I mean,' said Munroe.

'It's not a sensible way to try and do away with yourself,' said Rees.

Both policemen had seen the result of crashes in which cars left the road at sixty or seventy miles an hour and no one in them should have survived. But the facts contradicted these impressions. If God was on your side

He could throw you from the smouldering wreck, hurl you from a broken window before the metal crushed you, or tuck you down in some safe spot as your friends had their strings of life pulled apart like marionettes.

'What about the family? Anything there?'

'Nothing unusual. Grief, terrible tears from the mother. She's a bit too fond of the bottle these days, but no amount of gin would have helped her that day. The father's old-school, ex-military, a colonel, stiff upper lip. He doesn't show much, but he was devastated. They're one of the biggest families up here. Live in the Hall over at Llantrisillio. English, but they've been here generations. Our youngsters get killed in farming accidents, a tractor turns over, or they get caught up in the reeds, swimming in the mere on a hot summer's day. Their kid kills himself in his father's big car.'

'Was it just the three of them?'

'There's a girl. A younger sister, about fifteen or sixteen. She cracked up. Devoted to him. Older brother and all. It was me that went up to the Hall to tell them. Took Jane with me.'

'Jane?'

'The young WPC. You know, she was on the rustling team. She was here last night. All the lads fancy her. It was her first fatality. I took her along to help comfort the mother and daughter. But neither of them would let her near them. The mother broke down, just collapsed. They got the doctor to her. The girl wouldn't believe it, and then she just ran out of the room and down the drive. I could see her running full pelt, poor kid.'

'What was the lad doing in the car?'

'No one seemed to know. The old man didn't say much, but he couldn't understand why he was in it. Apparently the boy didn't usually use it. I got the feeling the old man didn't like anyone using it, really.'

'So where was he going?'

'No idea. In his pocket he had a bit of paper with some figures on it. It's with all his personal stuff in the evidence bag. It could have been anything. Some sort of calculations, I think. He had a few bob in change. A packet of fags, and some cigarette papers, but no tobacco. And that was it. Bit of a mystery what he was doing.'

'What did he do for a living?'

'He was at college in London. Art college. His father said he was up here on some sort of drawing holiday.'

'What about this, then? Any thoughts?' Munroe put the polythene bag with the ball of rubber gum in it on the table between them.

Rees picked it up, shrugged his shoulders and said, 'To hold the bonnet down? Maybe it was rattling, or loose or something. We'd better ask the old man.'

'Yes. Maybe. But what if this is *all* that was holding it down?'

'What? Fixed that way? But who wanted to hurt Charles Somerville?'

'Kill him, as it turned out.'

'Yes. Kill him.'

The landlord called 'time' and the two men went out to the urinal in the yard. It had the male, lunch-time pub smell of tobacco and beer and urine. They stood there, Munroe with a hand stretched out to the white-painted wall in front him, Rees looking down at the glazed trough as sodden cigarette ends floated past him.

CHAPTER SEVENTEEN

It started to drizzle as Munroe drove the few miles to Llantrisillio. The rain comforted him. He had walked a beat
often enough to know that it could be one of his best friends.
Small-time crooks stay indoors, perhaps not West End bank
robbers and airport heisters, but opportunist burglars.
Crime figures were always down in Birmingham on wet
weekends.

When he got to the village, he stopped on the bottom
lane and looked up the sweeping fields to the house itself.
The rain was falling heavily now, a steady, warm, May
downpour. He flicked the wipers on and off to swish the
water away and the windscreen demister whirred quietly
to clear the condensation inside.

The Hall looked sombre. It faced south and lay tucked
in beneath a fine stand of beech which was just losing its
grey austerity as it flushed into spring leaf. Like most of
the older houses in the district, it was built of the local
grey-blue stone which made it look cold and forbidding.
From two of the six tall chimneys, smoke funnelled up
through the steady downpour.

He wound down the window, dropped his cigarette stub
into the wet hedgerow and rattled over the cattle grid.

Rees had told him that Somerville did farm, but in a
faddish sort of way: he was unlikely, he said, to be found
laying land drains or planting corn. The ewes that grazed
the fields around Plas Trisillio were lawn-mowers and not,
primarily, beasts for market.

Munroe's car crunched to a halt on the gravel in front
of the porch on the west side. He pulled on the bell and
stood waiting for some minutes.

Eventually the door was opened by a small lady with striking black hair and opaque blue eyes.

'Good afternoon. Mrs Somerville? I'm John Munroe. Inspector Munroe. I'm sorry to trouble you, but I'm here to clear up a few points about your son's accident.'

Her gaze was unremitting. After an uncomfortably long pause Dorothea Somerville said, 'I see,' and turned away into the vestibule. Munroe stepped inside on to the cold, red quarry tiles.

She paused at the sheaf of letters and *The Times* that were still arranged neatly on the hall table. She fingered through the post, picked up none of it, and then shuffled down the dark passage.

Assuming that he was to accompany her, he followed. She disappeared through a big, squat door to the right and he followed her into the kitchen. It was painted in cream gloss, and had very high ceilings. The colour reminded him of the sort of young person's detention centre that he might have visited years ago. There was a copy of *Country Life* on the table and a cup with some coffee in it on a sideboard near the Aga. The saucer to the cup was on the table.

She peered into a mug, shook Nescafé into it from an open jar and then stood waiting by the electric kettle. He could see that it was not switched on. As if reading his mind, she pressed the switch. He waited rather awkwardly while they listened for the water to come to the boil.

Neither of them spoke and he looked around at the vast kitchen. It was an extraordinary mixture of 'modern' kitchen units that had not been fitted, either to one another or to the walls, and aged, dark, heavy furniture that had presumably been in the family for generations and would make a fortune at auction.

Next to a tall oak dresser with pink and white Worcester cups and saucers, plates and serving dishes randomly displayed upon it, was a cheap automatic washing-machine

which had wandered a foot away from the wall during the
course of completing its last cycle. There was a stack of
picture-moulding in one corner beside a long-range cobweb
remover, a few pheasant feathers tied to a six-foot piece of
cane. Hanging from the ceiling was a slatted wooden clothes
airer from which were suspended several shirts and a pair
of long pants.

On the dresser was a half-full bottle of French red wine,
and in the rack, several others. When she reached behind
her to get the milk from the refrigerator, he saw that there
was a bottle of vodka in there.

Before the kettle had come to the boil she poured the
water into his mug and put the coffee before him.

'Thank you,' he said.

She sat and he took the chair that was closest to him.
Her skin was very pale and had an unhealthy sheen, as if
she was never exposed to the fresh air. She was about five
feet four, wore loose, department-store jeans with a little
cotton blouse underneath a maroon jumper. Around her
shoulders hung a cardigan which was far too big for her.
She looked as if she needed several substantial meals and
a good night's sleep.

She looked directly at him, apparently ready to talk. Her
blue eyes had milky whites, like those of blind people. He
couldn't read what was there. She was detached, appeared
to have little interest in him nor in anything he was likely
to say. She was obviously still in shock, and he wished that
he had not come.

'Your son . . .' he began hesitantly.

'Yes?' she said, looking up at him.

'I *am* sorry, but I have to ask you a few questions
about . . .'

She looked at him, but still registered nothing.

'. . . about the circumstances in which he died,' he continued.

'A car crash,' she said.

'Yes. It was a car crash, of course.' He opened his note-book and scrutinized a blank page. 'Do you know where your son was going, Mrs Somerville? Or why?'

She looked at him and there was that unsettling pause again that somehow denied him the initiative in the questioning. 'No, I'm afraid I don't. Your colleagues have asked me the same question.'

'I see,' he said. 'But where *might* he have been going?' And, keen to encourage her, 'Shopping? To see a friend? A girlfriend, perhaps?'

'I really don't know,' she said. It was the 'really' that carried the message of dismissive superiority. She immediately tried to ameliorate the slight with a conciliatory, 'He was a grown-up young man, you know. He came and went . . .'

'Of course,' said Munroe, accepting the olive twig.

He drank some of his lukewarm coffee and a rotund little house dog waddled into the kitchen, completely ignored the policeman's presence and flopped down on the rug in front of the Aga.

He tried another approach. 'We can't understand why the car left the road. It shouldn't have done. It wasn't an old car. It was your husband's, I believe?'

'Yes,' she said.

'There was no other vehicle involved. Your son had not been drinking. The normal things that one looks for, perhaps expects to find . . . in this kind of situation. There seems to be a mystery.'

He hadn't asked a direct question but she was not responding to suggestion. He was beginning to flounder. She didn't help him. Perhaps she *was* in shock; maybe she *was* alcoholic, but she was making him feel ridiculous. His words sounded absurd. His Birmingham accent gross. It was a class difference. All his experience was worth nothing before people like this. *They* never doubted their place, and that made them unassailable. He felt uncouth and lumpen because she was wealthy and spoke well and shook the coffee from an open jar and didn't use a butter dish. The house was like a slum that had fallen about inside a museum. But people like this had nothing to prove. It was people like him who read the Sunday colour supplements and went to evening classes to learn things and percolated their coffee and preened their houses in pastel shades.

He was irked by her totally effortless superiority. He had come with sympathy and understanding and a wish to solve the apparent mystery of her boy's death. And now he felt resentful and antagonistic and was almost smug that she was grieving over her privileged son. But immediately he loathed himself for this callousness.

'Do you understand me, Mrs Somerville? What I'm saying is that we're not satisfied that your son's death *was* an accident.'

There was no gasp of shock or even acknowledgement from her. She said, 'I see,' and then, quietly, 'I'm going to have a drink. I don't suppose . . . ? You never do in the films . . .'

He was tempted to, just to contradict the convention, but he still had the alcohol of the previous night coursing in his veins, as well as the couple of pints from lunch-time. 'No, not for me, thank you. It's a bit early,' he lied.

There was a certain easing of the atmosphere as she played the red wine around the tumbler and then took frequent sips at it.

Without revealing the gum on the bonnet, he eventually spelled out for her his suspicions: it was possible that the car had been tampered with; if that was so, then the likely victim of any accident would have been the usual driver: her husband. Had she any idea of anyone who would wish to do the Colonel any harm? Business enemies? Had he dismissed any staff in the last year or two? Anything of the sort at all?

If she was non-committal when answering about her son, she was positively taciturn about her husband. There had been casual workers, she thought, people who came and went, seasonal employees, but no bad feeling of which she was aware. He would have to speak to her husband. She didn't know the details of what went on on the estate.

'Is your husband available?' he asked.

'He's gone to Scotland. To buy cattle. He's . . . trying to keep busy. It's his way of . . .' Her voice trailed away. 'He should be back in a day or two.'

Munroe said he would call back and see him sometime soon.

Before he left, he asked her permission to see her son's room.

'Of course,' she answered, and led him up the stairs to the door.

It had been tidied since the boy's death and, although his things were there, someone had folded his clothes and put them into the wardrobe and dressers; his books were stacked neatly on the desk beneath the window. The waste basket was empty; there was no towel on the oak, free-standing rail. It was now a room without an occupant, and told him little.

He thanked her for her time, offered his condolences again and left. The rain had stopped and the sun come out from a cleared sky.

As he walked to his car he was drawn by a noise from the stable-yard. Inside one of the boxes there was a rhythmic slapping and rubbing sound and it was some moments, stepping into the darkness of the stable out of the bright light of the yard, before he discerned a girl in Levi's and a man's checked shirt saddle-soaping the leather horse-tackle that she had spread over one of the partitions of the stalls.

She was working with absorption and he stood for a few seconds watching her as she rubbed the soap into the dark, damp leather.

He was about to turn and go, leaving her to her work, when she looked round. She stood up, arched her back and pushed the voluminous shirt into her jeans with one hand. She smiled and came towards him, beads of sweat on her brow, the wet, lathered sponge in her hand. 'Hello, I'm Susie. Are you looking for the Colonel?'

'Munroe. John Munroe,' he said, stepping forward and extending his hand. 'I was just talking to Mrs Somerville.' He paused, 'About Charles. Are you . . . you're not his sister are you?'

'No. I work here. With the horses. Part time, just a few hours a week.'

'I see.'

The girl took the initiative. 'It's a terrible thing.' She paused and frowned and looked at him, as if reminding him of the tragedy, 'About their son.'

'Yes,' he said feebly. He was charmed by her appearance. Her nose was a little large for her face and gave her a slightly gawky, unusual look that he liked. She had full lips and a fresh complexion with a few freckles around her nose. She wiped her forehead at last. There was a rip in the underarm of her shirt and he glimpsed the fair hair there.

'I'd hardly met him,' she said. 'I saw him a couple of times, just to say hello to. But we haven't been here long. He was home for a day or two. And then there was the . . . you know . . . the accident.'

She had a faint yellow bruise beneath her cheekbone. It could have been a birth mark of some sort, but he thought not. He wanted to ask her.

He took out his cigarettes. 'Do you mind?' he said.

'Not at all, but not in here . . . the straw and everything.'

'Of course,' he said. They walked to the door and he

offered her a Gold Leaf from his packet, but she declined.
They sat on the step together and she rolled a cigarette
from the tobacco tin in her shirt pocket.

'Are you a friend of the family?' she asked hesitantly.

'No. I'm a policeman.' And then, too soon, 'I'm making
a few inquiries.' He'd said this ten thousand times, but it
always sounded ridiculous.

'I see,' she said.

They each paid close attention to their cigarette-smoking.

'You're not from round here. Not with that accent,' she
said.

'You noticed!' he said, and they both laughed far too
extravagantly.

He didn't want to tell her that there were suspicious
circumstances about the boy's death. 'It's the normal sort
of thing after something like this. We have to check the car.
See if everything was all right. See that there's nothing
more . . .'

'Yes?' she said.

'Unusual . . . out of the ordinary.'

'And so you want to speak to the Colonel? He's away,
I'm afraid.'

'There's no hurry. I'll catch him sometime.' He got to
his feet, took off his jacket and slung it over his shoulder
in an exaggerated display of a casual demeanour. They
each had a damp patch on their outer thighs where her wet
sponge had sat between them on the step. 'I don't suppose
you've seen anything suspicious, have you? Anyone out of
the ordinary, heard anything odd, anything at all unusual?'

'This is the "normal sort of thing" is it?' she said, looking
at him knowingly.

'More or less,' he replied.

'We haven't been here long enough to know what *is*
usual. We'd only been here a few weeks when there was
that big rustling arrest. We left London to get away from

things, and suddenly, we're in the middle of this enormous police operation with people watching from hideouts with binoculars and car chases on the lane and roadblocks and God knows what.' She glanced away from him, surprised herself with the beginnings of a blush as she remembered making love to an exhausted James that night.

'It wasn't *quite* like that,' he said.

'Were you involved?' she asked, interested.

'Only a bit,' he replied modestly.

'Well, that's the way they tell it in the pub. Only I suppose it gets better at each telling! When the press were down here afterwards, they were throwing money around like mad, just to get anybody to say anything.'

'Yes, I bet. Was there anything else, though? Anyone around here? Any strange types? Anything at all that didn't look right to you?'

She played with her tobacco tin, rotated it slowly through her fingers, and pushed it up on her knee, and then round again, and up.

'Don't laugh.' She was quite stern with him and he liked the friendly little admonition that signalled a kind of understanding between them. 'But I did see something that I thought was strange. At least for round here.' She got to her feet, 'About a week ago, it must have been the day before Charles ... you know ... had his accident ... I was on my way to work here and I saw a big car parked on the bottom lane.'

'And?' he said.

'That's it. Just a big car with two men in it. And the driver was black. It did strike me as a bit unusual. I haven't seen any black people up here. Not one. I told you it was nothing.' She got up and started to walk with him towards the front of the house.

'Not at all,' he said. 'It could be useful. When you say it was a big car, do you know what it was?'

'I'm hopeless with cars. I can't tell one from another. But it was big. And it was blue. Dark blue.'

'Have a look at mine.'

They walked through the yard with its pleasant smell of sun after the shower on the red brick, and the sweet tang of the hay in the stalls.

As soon as she saw the Zephyr she laughed, 'No, it was a *really* big car. It was like . . . enormous. Much bigger than this. I don't think it was English. It was huge and low. Dark blue. I'm sorry. I said I was hopeless. I'm just not interested in cars, never have been. Look.' She pointed to her green and yellow Bedford van that was listing in the shade.

'Thanks, anyway,' he said. 'You never know what leads to something . . .'

'What is it you're looking for?' she asked seriously.

'It's nothing I can go into now. We just need to check a few things. I'd be glad if you'd not mention our having had a chat. It might be better.' She didn't answer but her look invited him to tell her more, and he was tempted. She looked so pretty and her eyes had a quick, trusting intelligence about them.

Something would not let him leave without asking. With one hand on the open car door, he lifted the other to her cheek, very close but not touching, 'What happened? Is it a bruise?'

'It's nothing,' she said evasively.

'Nothing?'

'A friend.'

Now *he* waited, unsatisfied. He wanted her to say more. She struggled for a form of words, but only repeated, 'It's nothing.'

He raised his eyebrows and got into the car as she stood there.

'What does your "friend" do? Does he live around here?'

The question was legitimate, but by no means disinterested.

'No, not any more,' she said.

He turned the key in the ignition and smiled at her. 'Good. I hope I'll see you again. Would you tell the Colonel that I called?'

'Sure,' she said, and watched him bump slowly away down the drive.

CHAPTER EIGHTEEN

Tony Rees was a nice man. He walked his dog, often read Gwennan, his youngest, her bedtime story, played football with Gwyn in the park on Sunday afternoons, and usually made the early morning tea on Saturdays. But he had his pride. And when Munroe, barely able to contain his excitement, led him into the corridor to spill his hot news about two strangers in a big car being in the area recently, Rees took a certain professional pleasure in dropping his Welsh wet blanket on the Birmingham man's news.

He already knew all about the two men, up from London in their blue Mercedes; everyone did. They had been like celebrities in the village pub at Llanfrynach where they had stayed. They were looking for a hotel, or a country club in the area. Londoners, a bit flash, but they seemed all right. They'd been here for a couple of nights, and then gone. Maybe they'd found what they were looking for, who knows?

'But when did they leave?' asked Munroe of the other man. 'When exactly?'

'I don't know, John,' said Rees, the use of his colleague's forename signalling his slight testiness at being questioned in this way. 'They'll be able to tell us at the Bear. Is there a connection, then?'

'I doubt it,' said Munroe. 'It's probably nothing, but I'll check them out.'

'How did you get on with Somerville?' asked Rees as the two men walked towards the office.

'He wasn't there. He's gone to bloody Scotland, won't be back for a couple of days. But I spoke to his missus. Didn't get anywhere at all with her. What's going on there?'

'Nothing! Somerville's been playing away for years. George Fry's wife over at Llandrinio.'

'Who's Fry?' said Munroe.

'Solicitor in Shrewsbury. Has his own practice, biggest in the county,' replied Rees.

'Bloody hell, Far from the Madding Crowd . . .' muttered Munroe. 'And does he know?'

'Do I?' said Rees laconically.

'And he doesn't mind?'

'He has his own particular . . . friends, so they say.'

'I see. And Mrs Colonel? What about her?' asked Munroe.

'I think her comfort comes out of a bottle these days. A shame. She used to be the belle of the ball. You can still just see it on her good days.'

'Why didn't you tell me this before I went up there?' said Munroe, chagrined.

'You were in such a hurry.' Rees tapped his nose, 'Local knowledge, you see, John. Local knowledge.'

'Touché,' said Munroe.

Munroe went up to the empty, quiet snooker room on the first floor of the police station. It was a good table. Plenty of nap on the baize, well-brushed, and neatly cut pockets. He took off his jacket and put the colours on their spots. The regulars' cues were hung in their metal tubes, each one padlocked and named, but even the guest cues in the rack were good: all ash, with long, even grain and good, well shaped, rounded tips.

He flipped his notebook on to the window-sill, lit a cigarette and laid it in the ashtray; the blue smoke curled up in the sunlight.

Perhaps the Colonel had had a minor bump? Someone had reversed into him while parking, or he had run into a car in a traffic queue.

His right leg rigid, he crooked his left, playing the cue through his bridge and potted the yellow off its spot. The white ran through sweetly for the green.

He had stuck a bit of gum between the bonnet and the grille to stop the movement or rattle.

He overhit the green and it juddered in the jaws before dropping in. The white followed through and stopped tight up against the cushion. Only two shots and his game was starting to come apart. He hit the brown full on and the white fouled into the centre pocket.

And he had 'killed' his own son?

He re-spotted the white and met the brown and the cushion perfectly, the ball hugging the side and dropping into the far pocket.

It could have been the Colonel himself. But if someone *had* bumped his car, he would have told the police by now?

He played the long blue and missed it by a mile.

He needed to speak to him. But he was in Scotland, and Munroe couldn't wait. He also had a nagging doubt about Londoners who arrived in the sticks to look for hotels at the same time as wealthy youngsters died in mysterious circumstances.

He laid his cue on the table and picked up his jacket. The Gold Leaf cigarette burned on in the ashtray. If Somerville had had only a minor bump, either the local garage or his insurance broker would probably know. Downstairs in the back office he phoned the Rover main dealer in Shrewsbury.

The service manager consulted his records and reported that the car had received all its services: one, a post-delivery check; a fifteen-hundred-mile running-in check; and then three-thousand-mile services, always within a few hundred miles of the due time. There was no damage to the car when they had serviced it two months ago and there had been no other communication from Colonel Somerville since that time. Munroe thanked him for his time and rang off.

He checked the plastic wallet of documents that had been taken from the car's glove compartment, and telephoned the Colonel's insurance broker. The broker knew about the fatality, but apart from this terrible tragedy there had been no insurance claim of any sort during the last twelve years.

When he had run off the Inspector wondered if, for whatever reason, Somerville might have put a claim through direct to the insurance company. It was possible. He might have opened his file, seen the company's name and rung them direct, especially in the heat of the moment, after a little accident, for example.

The receptionist at Northern Star put him through to claims and a girl there sent him back to inquiries as it wasn't a current claim but an inquiry about whether one had been lodged. That would be filed in another department. En route around the huge building in Manchester, he was cut off and had to dial again. This time he got through to the right place. As the woman on the other end of the line made clear rather sniffily, most people knew whether they had a claim against an insurance company without having to telephone to find out. He told her again that he was a policeman and was involved in an investigation. She was unimpressed and he heard the receiver hit the desk as she went off to check his inquiry.

He could hear that the other girls in the office were going to Sandra's hen party that Friday, but still hadn't decided what to buy for her with the thirty-five shillings that they had collected in the department. After a few minutes he heard the shuffle of papers as Mrs Connell picked up the receiver.

'Hello. We've no record of any claim against that name.' She frowned at the silence from the other end of the phone. The Inspector was irked.

'Hello, are you still there? Was there something else?'
she asked haughtily.

Munroe dropped the receiver into its cradle.

CHAPTER NINETEEN

The next morning, while Rees was in court giving evidence on a burglary case, Munroe used the Yellow Pages and turned up the addresses of the half-dozen garages within a few miles' radius of Llantrisillio.

It was pleasant enough police work, tootling around on a warm May day, introducing himself to one-man garage owners with greasy hands, and asking them if they had ever done any work on Colonel Somerville's black Rover.

They all knew the man. It was a community that knew everyone in it for twenty miles around. But none of the garages that he called at had ever done more than sell the Colonel a few gallons of petrol.

Munroe had that sensation of looking for the lost cricket ball: of course you have to look in the hedge, just here, but all the time there is the suspicion that the object of the search may be somewhere else entirely, all your time here being completely wasted.

He pulled on to the forecourt of the fourth garage on his list, Geraint Lewis's two-pump, corrugated-iron workshop affair on the edge of the village of Llansillin. It was twelve noon, lunch-time, and the owner was sprawled at the doors of his workshop in a seat that he had removed from an Armstrong-Siddley years ago. It was a massive brown leather thing the size of an armchair. The man looked up from his local paper and watched closely as Munroe walked towards him. He made no attempt to move or greet the policeman. When Munroe was close enough to see the depression that the man's dirty fingers had made in the white bread sandwich in his hand, the garageman volunteered a ''Morning.'

''Morning,' said Munroe, 'lovely day.' He was learning.
A month ago and he would have already asked his questions
and been driving away by now. But in the short time that
he had been working here he had learned to adjust his
interrogatory clock. He said no more, half turned his back
on the man lounging in the chair and took in the view of
the Carno Hills in front of him.

Lewis watched closely as Munroe, caricaturing a tourist,
breathed in the vista. He had not himself consciously looked
at the hills for months. They were as much a part of his
landscape as the baked bean tins and cereal packets on a
grocer's shelves are to a grocer: sometimes they were green,
sometimes blue or mauve or filled with black clouds and
rain; sometimes covered with snow in March, but always
they were just there.

Eventually, the corpulent man's curiosity triumphed.
'What can I do for you?' he drawled. Munroe had won the
first round.

'Just an inquiry,' said the policeman nonchalantly. He
turned and showed the man his warrant card. The garageman peered at it and was still trying to examine it as
Munroe folded it away.

He struggled out of the low chair and got to his feet.
'What is it, then?' he asked.

'Only routine. Colonel Somerville's car. I wondered if
you'd ever done any work for him?'

'Colonel Somerville,' repeated the man slowly 'Lives at
the Hall at Llantrisillio? His boy died in that terrible crash?'

'That's right,' said Munroe, 'that's him.'

'I don't think we've ever done any work for him. I suppose he goes to Brian Davies in Llanfrynach, if he goes
anywhere local. That would be the nearest. Have you
spoken to Brian?'

'Brian Davies . . . Llanfrynach . . .' Munroe looked at his
notebook. 'Yes, I've seen him. He says he never did any

work on the car I'm interested in. It was the big Rover.'

'The one that his boy died in?' said the Welshman, sniffing the possibility of someone else's wrong-doing and the chance that he might himself benefit in some as yet undefined way.

'It's just a routine inquiry. You know, when something like this has happened, we have to check everything.'

'Of course,' said the man, conspiratorially.

'Do you have anyone else to help you here?'

'Only me and the wife. There's no call for more than that.'

'No one else?' said Munroe, dejected.

'Just a lad on Saturdays.'

'Right,' said Munroe. He wandered over and looked in at the dark workshop with its trolley jacks, oil cans, spanners, sockets and pile of used batteries in the corner. The pit was covered with a line of oily railway sleepers. 'Thanks for your help,' he said, and walked towards his car.

The man followed him, the sandwich held slightly away from his chest in his dirty hand. Now that the policeman was going, and his own impunity was assured, he wanted to play a part, be involved, 'Just Saturday mornings . . .' he offered.

Munroe got into his car and started to pull the door to. 'Sorry?' he said.

'He doesn't work Saturday afternoons. Plays for Llantrisillio. Centre-forward. He's always in the paper. Scores bloody goals every week.'

'Good,' said Munroe, not even bothering to feign interest.

The window was half way down. The man was looking in. The Inspector wound it all the way and rested his arm on the sill. He started the engine. 'Good afternoon.'

The man took a step back from the car.

Munroe disengaged the gear. 'Just for the record . . .'

Lewis looked at him vacantly.

'I'd better have his name. For the record.' He took his notebook from the passenger seat and propped it against the steering-wheel. Lewis thrust his head in the open window. His breath smelled of cheese and onion. Munroe averted his face and wrote down the boy's name. The man wasn't sure of the number of the council house where he lived, but there were only a dozen in the block, and Peter Ryan's was the one by the lamp post. You couldn't miss it.

'Thanks,' said Munroe.

'It's a pleasure,' Lewis said earnestly, as the Inspector pushed the column change up into first. As he drove out of earshot, Lewis shouted, 'Anything I can do, sir. Any time.'

Back at the station, Rees had left a message that he would be back at about six. Munroe went to the filing cabinet and took out again the notes on the boy's post-mortem. He scanned them, and picked up the phrase that had troubled him the first time that he had seen it: 'Left calf, deep laceration, unlikely to have been caused by trauma sustained in fatal car crash.'

The crash had happened over a week ago and, as far as the pending inquest was concerned, there were no suspicious circumstances. Apart from reporting the fatality to them, and his own inconclusive visit yesterday, no one had yet questioned Charles's family. More importantly, the police had seen no reason to visit the boy's London address.

According to Dorothea Somerville, no one from the family had yet been there. Her husband intended to go to the boy's flat and bring his things home next week, after the inquest.

Munroe knew that if there was anything to see, any clue as to why someone might wish to harm the boy, he had to see the flat now. It was nearly three in the afternoon. The last thing he wanted to do was start the two-hundred-mile drive to London.

On Rees's desk he left a note, 'Gone South, young man. Will call you later, John.'

At Montford Bridge on the River Severn he filled up the Zephyr with four star and headed down the A5 towards Wolverhampton. The light was beginning to fade and the thunderous trucks were rumbling down the black tarmac road to the industrial Midlands and beyond. He slotted into the rhythm and began to weave in and out of the traffic, just this side of danger. He felt resigned.

He stopped for coffee and a warm grey pasty on the M6 outside Birmingham and listened to the desultory chat and music on the car radio. He smoked to try and stay alert. The ashtray was overflowing. At Hendon he narrowly avoided a rear-end shunt as he searched the glove compartment for the London *A to Z*.

He had missed the rush hours, and it was still too early for people's evenings out, so the roads were quiet. With the *A to Z* that refused to stay open propped on his knee, one finger trailing the grey lines, he skirted Regent's Park, crossed wide Marylebone Road and headed for Chelsea. He found the flat in Elm Park Road and arrived at just gone eight.

He pressed the bell at the front door and heard the faint ring in the distance, through a couple of doors and up a flight of stairs. He opened the heavy door with the key that he had taken from the plastic bag of the dead boy's belongings at the station.

There was a timer on a push button for the light on the staircase and he depressed it and went up to the first floor. The words 'Charles Somerville' were printed on a cardboard slip, and pinned to the door surround of the first-floor flat. With the Yale key he opened the door.

The flat had a musty and stale air about it. He switched on the lights. He felt more like a thief than a policeman.

The place was in disarray. Had the boy left in a hurry? A real hurry? Did he live in this kind of mess always? Someone had surely been here after him. But there was no sign of a forced. Maybe someone had a key. A friend? His girl?

The mess was the kind of thing he had seen at countless professional burglaries. Not the out and out destruction by kids after they had lifted the bit of cash and jewellery, but the methodical turning over of the absent resident's possessions. Of course pro's didn't fold things up and put them back in the drawers, but at least they didn't chuck flour about and urinate in the back of the television set.

Munroe was delighted that the place had been gone over: unless it was a random burglary it meant that someone had an interest in Charlie and his flat and his doings which might give substance to the Inspector's hunch about his death.

He opened the refrigerator. The milk was off. There was a cup of tinned tomatoes which had developed a gauzy green fungus. The butter was rancid. Although the boy had died only a week ago, he had been in Llantrisillio for two or three days before that, and the flat appeared to have been unoccupied at least since then.

On the table by the window, among the junk mail and art books, was a London *Evening Standard* dated Friday the twenty-sixth of April.

It was open at the car ad's. As he dropped it back on the table, he noticed a faint pencil ring around a couple of the cars among the hundreds listed there. He put the paper in his jacket pocket.

As he opened the door to the windowless bathroom, an automatic fan started to whirr on the far wall. He stood at the door and watched the regular drip of the cold tap in the bath that had left a green mark over the years. On the tiled floor there was talc and dust and a knot of hair that someone had pulled from a hairbrush and let fall where they had stood.

In the bedroom he rifled through the clothes and drawers. There was a piece of cannabis in the bedside cabinet, and he recalled the cigarette papers and cigarettes in the evidence bag.

He took a last look, turned off the lights, and closed the door of the flat behind him. In the bathroom, the fan continued to whirr, and the little knot of hair moved back and forth on the floor.

Downstairs, the girl from the ground-floor flat was waiting for him. She had heard his movements in the flat above. She was a little afraid of confronting him, but as soon as she saw him on the stairs she knew that she had nothing to fear. He looked tired, but there was no aggression in his brown eyes. 'Hello,' he said.

'Hi,' she replied, and took a step back from the banister where she was waiting.

'Do you live here?' he asked.

'Yes, in there.' She pointed to the door behind her in the hall. 'Are you looking for Charlie?'

He didn't know what to answer. Charlie was on a cold slab two hundred miles away. 'Not exactly,' he said.

'You don't want to see him, "exactly", but you're in his flat for half an hour.' She drew back. 'Who are you? What do you want Charlie for?'

He drew out his warrant card. 'I'm a policeman. Charlie's had an accident, I'm afraid.'

'What kind of accident?'

'In a car.'

'Is he all right?' she said, concerned.

'Do you think we could . . . ?' and he indicated the door to her flat.

She hesitated but then led them into the ground-floor room that looked out on to the road.

The room smelled of incense and there was a pink scarf draped around the table lamp in the corner; there were some spindly plants that were probably cannabis standing by the window. He had seen plenty of rooms like it over the years. Every little drug bust that he had been on took place somewhere just like this. He had seen the magazines on the floor and the records on the shelves and the posters on the wall: Hendrix and Pink Floyd and The Doors. He'd seen the facile aphorisms that exorted the world to turn on, tune in and drop out; that the longest journey began with the first footstep; that the Hobbits lived in Middle Earth; and that if you joined the army you could travel the world, meet interesting people, and kill them.

Over the marble mantelpiece was a print of one of the maxims of Kahlil Gibran:

You give but little when you give of your possessions.
It is when you give of yourself that you truly give.
For what are your possessions but things you keep and guard for
fear you may need them tomorrow?

They sat opposite one another either side of the fireplace. 'When did you last see Charlie?' he asked her, as she lit a cigarette.

She ignored the question, and insisted, 'What's happened to him?'

'Look,' he said, 'tell me what you know, and then I'll tell you all I can.'

She looked at him carefully and then, resigned, began, 'He came in, packed a couple of bags and left. I saw him go. I was with a friend of mine, we'd just got in from a gig at the Roundhouse. It was Friday night, well, four or five in the morning. Charlie came to the front, went upstairs,

and half an hour later he was gone. We were sitting in the
window watching the dawn come up. He just waved and
went.'

'Was he in a car?'

'Yes.' She sat forward and knocked the ash from her
cigarette into the cold marble hearth, 'That was weird,
I'd never seen him driving. I didn't even know he *could*
drive.'

'What kind of car was it?' he asked, without expectation.

'An Austin 1100. Sherwood Green, 'E' registered; it must
have been a '65.'

He thought that she was having some sort of joke at his
expense. 'Are you a student of cars, Miss . . . ?'

'Tudor. Elaine Tudor. And no, I'm not. But I've got
two brothers who are. And if you'd spent as many Sunday
afternoons and holidays as I have driving with a father and
two brothers who are identifying every last feature of every
new car that they pass on the road, you'd either end up
totally mad, or as knowledgeable as I am!'

He smiled, and looked around the room with its posters
and records, books and plants. It was a world away from
the one that she had just alluded to. His look said to her,
'And all this?'

She shrugged and said, 'Old habits die hard,' and then,
seriously, 'What kind of accident has he had?'

'He had a car crash; a very bad one. I'm afraid he's
dead.'

'Oh no!' she said, and her eyes filled with tears. 'How?
Where?'

'Near his home, in Wales. Shortly after he arrived there.
He lost control of the car on a bend.'

'I don't know what to say,' she offered. She had never
known anyone who had died; her grandparents were all
alive.

After some moments' silence she was glad when Munroe

began again, 'I'm sorry to ask you questions, but I have to know . . .' His faltering voice and hesitation was a sham, a respectful pretence of grief. His own emotional feelings had, for several days now, been replaced by an intense curiosity about the real reasons for the boy's death.

'Has anyone been to see him during the last few days?' he asked.

She knew that Charlie dealt drugs, there were a few callers at the flat every week. 'One or two,' she answered evasively. 'Friends . . .'

He sniffed the hesitation. 'Anyone in particular?'

She was trying to connect the unpleasant man on the stairs a week ago, and his chilling statement, 'We'll be seeing him,' as he took Charlie's letters from the post-box, with a car accident now.

She had learned to be wary of the police, but she knew that the man she had seen on the stairs that day looked more like her idea of a real criminal than the kind of people who were outside the law because they smoked a bit of dope or dropped an acid tab at weekends.

'A man did come. A day or so after Charlie left. He didn't look very nice. You know, sharp suit and mean face. He was wearing a big gold watch. He came in the evening, in a Mercedes. Another guy was driving. I couldn't see the driver. The man went into Charlie's flat. I was afraid of him and all he said to me when he left was, "We'll be seeing him." He was a frightening guy.'

Munroe took a detailed description from Miss Tudor of the man she had seen.

'Anyone else?' he asked.

'No one special. Just the usual people. His friends from the college, that kind of thing.' And then she added involuntarily, 'This is terrible. It's so awful.'

He said, 'Yes, I'm sorry,' in his most maudlin voice. In fact, he couldn't wait to pursue the men in the German car

and find out what they were really doing in Montgomeryshire at the same time as the son of the local land-owner
was dying.

As he left he gave her his telephone number and, at the
metal grille that held the letters, removed the half-dozen
that were addressed to Charles. 'Thanks for your help,' he
said.

''Bye,' she said, and managed a wan smile.

CHAPTER TWENTY

At a fake velvet and brass pub around the corner from Charles's flat, Munroe took out the *Evening Standard* that he had taken.

The first pencil ring circled a '1965 Mini, cloth upholstery, 26,000 miles, good condition, £325.00 o.n.o.,' a Kensal Rise telephone number.

The other was a 1966 Austin 1100. 'One owner, low mileage, VGC, £395. No offers.' Very severe, thought Munroe, 'No offers,' indeed. It was a Wimbledon number.

He bought another pint of the gassy Worthington beer and tried not to slip off the red nylon plush seat. So why had Charlie Somerville bought a car the day before he left London? Had he needed to move something? Had he needed to get out fast? Get away from men who came to his flat, and then followed him a couple of hundred miles to the Welsh borders? Faster than he could have done travelling by train? And where was the car now?

In the corridor that led to the gents' there was a payphone on the wall. He phoned Welshpool. The contrary desk sergeant told him that Rees had gone home. But he'd left a message. There was a pause while the playful sergeant waited for Munroe to ask him what it was. 'He said, "Thanks for your message; no message."'

'Thanks,' said Munroe, and replaced the receiver.

He dialled the Mini at the Kensal Rise number and a woman answered.

'I'm sorry to phone so long after the advert was in,' he began, 'but I've been away for a few days. Do you still have the car for sale?'

There was no response from the other end, but the phone

hung from its cord and bounced on the wall as he heard, 'Dec . . . lan . . . There's someone on the phone about the car.'

He heard the thump-thump of stairs being descended rapidly.

'Hello? Hello, is it about the car?' The speaker had a soft southern Irish burr, a young man's voice.

'Yes,' said Munroe. 'Do you still have it?'

'I do. Someone said they were coming round to see it but never turned up.' There was a pause. 'It's a good car. Never let me down.'

Munroe tried to sound interested. All he wanted to know was if Charles had been to see it, or phoned. He asked the first thing that came into his head, 'How many owners has it had?'

'I'm the third,' came the dispirited reply.

'Thanks, that's fine,' said Munroe, stalling. 'I'll call back when I've had a word with my wife.'

'Sure,' said the Irishman.

'One thing,' said Munroe, just before the man could hang up. 'A friend told me about your car. I think he may have phoned you about a week ago.'

'So?' said the Irishman.

Someone pushed past him in the corridor on their way to the toilets. 'He didn't buy it . . . obviously . . . but I think he phoned you . . . Do you remember him, I wonder, a well-spoken young man . . . ?'

'Look, do you want to see the car or not? Loads of people phoned. No one bought it. It's still for sale. Do *you* want it? Do you even want to see it? Or do you want something else?'

'I'm sorry,' said the Inspector, 'it's just that . . .' and before he could continue, the phone at the other end of the line was slammed down.

He went to the gents' and when he got back to the phone

a girl was using it. He stood as far away from her as he could, while at the same time letting her know that he was waiting to make a call. She twirled the cord around her arm as she talked quietly in the narrow corridor. Eventually her mumble became more audible and animated. The end of the conversation. He approached. She replaced the receiver without even glancing at him. 'Thank you,' he said unnecessarily.

He got through to the Wimbledon number and a woman answered. She was wary, even with the safety of a phone line between them. She had a northern accent, Lancashire. Were there any Londoners in London, he wondered.

He guessed from her voice that she was in her early twenties. She was sorry, the car was sold. It had been sold on the first night that she had advertised it.

Munroe told her that he was a policeman and needed to know about the buyer. Her tone changed immediately. He sought to reassure her. No, there was nothing wrong with the car.

'Incidentally, what colour was it?' he asked.

'Why?' she retorted, surprised and rather defensive.

'Please,' he said, patronizingly, 'what colour was it?'

'Sherwood green. What exactly are you trying to find out?' she asked.

He decided to come clean, or at least tell her half the truth. 'There's nothing wrong with the car, but the buyer may be related to an inquiry that we are pursuing. We need to know about his movements. Anything that he did in the last week or two might help us with the picture. It won't take long, I assure you. Just a couple of questions.'

She agreed before she realized that he meant he would need actually to see her. She gave him the address and insisted that she would not speak to him unless he had identification.

Just across the road from the pub he stepped into the

unworldly yellow light of a late night florist's. He picked up some freesias and put them to his nose, but all he could smell was the beer and tobacco on his own breath. Daffodils and narcissi were everywhere. The pink tulips caught his eye but they were still in tight bud, and he only liked them when, in the warmth, they opened themselves to reveal their mysterious insides. He settled for blue and yellow iris.

The florist took the details. 'They'll be there first thing tomorrow morning,' said the lady. Her greasy, orange foundation and red lips looked surreal in the yellow light. 'What message?' she said, her ballpoint poised above a little greetings card.

'Just say, "To Kath. With my love," please.' And, as an afterthought, 'No Cellophane or spray with them. Just the flowers, wrapped in paper. Is that all right?'

'Certainly,' she said, rather haughtily. He seemed to think that it was *these* flowers that would be delivered to the address in Birmingham the following morning!

He drove south across Putney Bridge and out through pleasant Roehampton into Wimbledon. No. 34 Oldfield Road was a terraced house in one of those forgotten little streets off Wimbledon Park Road.

Built at the turn of the century in red brick, each house in the short street had a tiny bay window, most of which had furtively parted from the main structure as they sank into the inadequate foundations of the London clay. There was a neat box hedge at No. 34 and behind it, the original leaded, stained glass front door.

She checked his identification carefully, stepping out into the front porch to do so. When she was satisfied that he was who he said he was she let him down the hallway and into a kitchen which had been opened up and now incorporated the larder and old wash-house to make a spacious, airy room. There were French windows leading out on to a paving-slab patio with a dozen plant pots filled with primulas and bunches of daffodils that had been tied up as they started to die back.

She had fair, straight hair cut quite short. He thought he might have heard it called a 'choir boy'. Or was it 'page boy'? She wore spectacles and smart office clothes, a blue skirt and a nice cream shirt; the jacket was draped over a chair, but carefully, not to crease it.

She stood at the tidy work surface and made them coffee.

'You said on the phone that you sold the car straight-away?' he said.

'Yes. He was the first person to see it.'

'Was this him?'

She put the cups and tea-towel down and squinted at the black and white photograph of a young man outside a riverside pub. He was acting the fool, hands around the neck of a pretty eighteen-year-old in a summer dress.

'Yes, that's him, I'm sure that's him.' She handed the photograph back to the Inspector, was uncomfortable with the picture of the happy, slightly out of focus couple, to whom something, she felt certain, must have happened. 'What's he done? Has he been involved in something?'

'He's had an accident.'

It confirmed her fears. 'In my car?' she said, shocked and afraid.

'No. There's no problem with the car that you sold him. At least, as far as we know there isn't. I haven't actually seen your car. That's one of the things I'd like to know. Where it is. Why he bought it, and where he went in it.'

She asked him if the boy was all right. He avoided answering her.

'How did he seem, when he came here? Did he seem all right?'

'Yes, I think so. He looked at the car, started it up, looked under the bonnet, and bought it. The only thing he asked me was if it was all right. He took my word for it. And it was,' she added defensively.

'How did he get here?'

'What do you mean?'

'Did he come on his own or did someone bring him?'

'Well, he was on his own when he looked at the car. I suppose he came on the tube. Wimbledon Park station's only round the corner. And the bus stops on the High Street. He can't have come by car, because when he'd counted the money out, I gave him the log book and he drove off.'

'Did he say why he was buying it?'

'No.'

'Was there anything strange about him or the way he was behaving? Did he seem agitated? Worried?'

'No, I don't think so. He seemed all right. He was rather nice, actually. He spoke well. You know, well-educated. He was wearing jeans and desert boots, but like a well-off student, really.'

'How did he pay?'

'I told you, in cash.'

'How exactly? What notes?'

'Tens and fives. I paid them into my building society the next morning.'

They drank another cup of coffee and chatted in a desultory way. She was in London from Stockport, shared the house with two other girls. They were all doing well-paid secretarial work, and spending their money on clothes and going to the films and shows. They were having a good time.

He made a note of the registration number of the 1100 as he stood beside her at the front door. She asked again what had happened to the boy. He was tired and had no resistance to her question. 'He had an accident. Nothing to do with your car. I'm afraid he's dead.'

'Oh God, how terrible,' she said.

'I'm sorry,' he muttered. 'I'm sorry.'

He walked the two steps to the pavement and she closed the door quietly behind him. He looked back and saw her shape through the glazed door making its way down the hall.

He drove on to the North Circular at Richmond and wound up to Hendon Way, just short of the start of the M1. He was exhausted. It was impossible to drive up to Birmingham, his eyes were closing. He pulled in at a busy lay-by, locked the doors and climbed over the bench seat into the back of the car. With his coat pulled around him and the traffic rumbling by, he fell asleep.

CHAPTER TWENTY-ONE

There was a tapping outside the car. He wiped the condensation from the window and saw the traffic booming past. The tapping continued. It was insistent, it was saying, 'I'm here, this side.' He ran his shirtsleeve across that window. There was a pretty young face, eighteen or nineteen years old, framed by a head of long dark hair.

He leaned towards the handle and flipped it up. His back was hell. The girl opened the door, stood back and said, 'Are you going to Birmingham?'

The air in the closed car was fetid. He ached from his neck to his ankles. 'Uuum,' he groaned.

'Does that mean yes?' she insisted. She was urgent in her demands.

'Yes, sure. Just give me a few minutes.'

'OK,' she said, and took another step back from the car.

He stretched his neck and back, put on his shoes but didn't lace them, his feet had grown half a size during the night. He creaked up and down the lay-by and stamped his soles to get rid of the pins and needles. The place was already full of trucks and conversations between men who had been driving all night and were already in animated possession of the day.

He urinated behind the dusty hedge, full of sweet wrappers and worse and shivered in the early May sunshine.

The girl got into the front seat with him and they drove off towards the motorway. She wore an Indian cotton skirt, tie-dyed T-shirt and short, rather smelly Afghan coat. She was talkative. She'd hitched to here this morning. It was easy. She'd got family in Birmingham, was going up to see them. She lived with friends in a communal house in Notting Hill. She did a bit of bar work or waitressing if she needed money, but on the whole, she just hung out, 'taking what's mine,' as she put it. She talked, he listened. It wasn't yet eight a.m.

She asked him what he did but hardly waited to hear the answer. He thought it politic not to be too specific and his comment that he worked 'for the government' was lost in her next tirade. She was becoming quite animated. She was an anarchist, a soldier in the class war. The enemy was everywhere: landlords; the electricity and gas companies; tax officials; car owners; shop keepers, from whom goods had to be liberated, and anyone with money in the bank. All these people were, by definition, corrupt and dishonest. But it was the police who were the subject of her most virulent attack. They were the real plague of a free society: uniformed automata who were sworn to secret oaths and who would use any means to intimidate and destroy freedom fighters like herself.

He advanced a token argument or two, but she had answers to everything he could summon. Of course there wouldn't be civil disorder and rape and pillage without law enforcement; that was an argument put about by the present repressive law-makers and their capitalist lackeys, the judiciary.

He wanted to declare a truce; his head was splitting and he needed a cup of coffee. He admitted that he'd met some nasty cops in his time, but he'd also met unpleasant crane-drivers and labourers and teachers and shop assistants; he wasn't convinced, he offered weakly, that the cops had a monopoly on malevolence.

They stopped at the Blue Boar service station and he bought her coffee and a slice of apple tart. When he asked her if she thought that it might be dangerous to hitch-hike, a young girl, alone, she said that she could look after herself.

'And anyway,' she added, almost as if *he* were in some way to blame for today's act of industrial anarchy, 'I've no choice: the trains are on strike again.'

She thought that she must have offended him. He got up from the table abruptly, left his coffee cup half full and rushed towards the door. 'I won't be a minute,' he called back to her. A couple of the truck-drivers looked up from their bacon and beans and fried eggs.

He leaned into the back seat of the car where the *Evening Standard* that he had taken from Charlie's flat lay. From the car ad's page he turned to the front page. Beneath the date, Friday, 26th April, the banner headline shouted, MORE RAIL MISERY TODAY.

He rejoined his bemused companion and gave her a warm smile. 'Thanks,' he said. 'Another coffee?'

She looked at him warily, 'If you like,' she said.

He cleaned his teeth in the gents' toilet and bought a newspaper. He thought the *Guardian* might interest her, but as soon as she had scanned the headlines, she threw the paper into the back seat, dismissing it with the words 'capitalist propaganda press'.

'The *Guardian*?' he said, rather abashed that his attempt at détente had been rejected.

'They're all in league,' she informed him. 'Just under different banners to give the illusion of press freedom.'

'It's an orchestrated policy?' he asked.

'Of course,' she said contemptuously, 'The only people who tell the truth in this country are the underground press.' And she pulled from her pocket a pamphlet entitled *Anarchy*.

Her view of the press was not negotiable and, with the pamphlet clutched in her fist, she glared out of the window so as not to miss the oppression being wrought on the proletariat in the streets of Watford and Hemel Hempstead.

The tacitly confrontational atmosphere gave him the

chance that he needed to reflect on the case: Charles Somerville had left London at dawn a little over a week ago. He had been seen leaving in a car that he had bought the previous evening from a lady in Wimbledon. He had paid £395 for it, in cash. He had arrived at his home the following day, telling his parents that he had travelled by train. In fact, the trains, having been on strike, were disrupted. Since he had left London, two men in a Mercedes had been to his flat looking for him.

Shortly after Charlie had arrived in Montgomeryshire, a couple of strangers in a Merc had stayed at the village pub; but two days later, very soon after Charles had died driving his father's car, they had left. The car in which Charles had died had almost certainly been tampered with.

He was still deep in thought as they approached Birmingham on the M6. 'What part of Birmingham does your family live?' he asked.

'Erdington,' she said sullenly.

'I'm going to Handsworth,' he replied. 'I'll let you off at Gravelly Lane. You can take a bus from there. It's not far.'

'I'm going to Erdington,' she said sharply.

There was something distinctly unpleasant in her tone. Something that he had not heard before, even at her most persecuted and zealous.

'Well, I'm going to Handsworth. That's as far as I'm taking you,' he said sternly.

She pulled up her long, mauve skirt with one hand and pushed her fingers into the waistband of her knickers with the other. 'You're taking me to Erdington, or you'll be in court for trying to rape me. And I want some money. If you haven't got twenty quid on you, stop at a bank and get it.' She didn't look at him, looked straight ahead out of the windscreen.

He pulled off the motorway and drove through Castle Bromwich and into Handsworth. Instead of going down

Soho Road and out towards Erdington, he pulled up abruptly outside the old red-brick police station in Holly Lane.

She looked up at the police station and sneered, 'You think I'm kidding.'

'No, I don't think you're kidding.' He pulled his warrant card out of his pocket and held it close to her face. 'Get the fuck out of my car, you tramp.'

'You bastard,' she said.

'I'm just glad it was me instead of some other poor fucker. Go on, piss off. Up the revolution!'

There was no one in at Coleraine Road. Two days' milk was on the front doorstep and a bunch of iris was propped up in the corner of the porch. It was wrapped in Cellophane and had a bunch of spray with it. On the floor inside the door was some post.

He went through to the kitchen. He called, to make sure, but he knew the sounds of an empty house, 'Kath . . . Kath . . .'

He took a cup from the draining-board, swilled it under the tap and spooned coffee into it. After he had put the kettle on he went through to the phone in the hall.

'Rees? This is John here. Tony, is that you? It's a very bad line.' He could barely hear the Welshman through the crackle of static all the way to Welshpool Police Station.

'What's going on, John? Where are you?' said Rees.

'I'm at home, in Birmingham. I've been to London to see the boy's place. I think we're on to something. Can you hear me, Tony? You sound as if you're in a foreign country! You have got the phones connected properly up there, have you?!'

'I can hear you, boyyo, forget the bloody jokes. What have you got, then?'

'It might be nothing. But he bought a car. The evening

before he left London. A girl at his flat saw him drive off in it. But his mother says he came home by train.'

'You can't rely on her, John,' Rees shouted down the line, 'I told you, she sees everything through the bottom of a glass.'

'I know, but she seemed sure enough on this. The boy told them he'd come up by train that morning. But he *can't* have come by train, Tony. They were bloody well on strike.'

'Of course they were,' said Rees. 'Good work, John. So where's the car?'

'God knows!' said Munroe.

'Where do you want me to start?'

'Anywhere you can think of,' said Munroe, and he gave him the details of the 1100. 'And give Swansea DVLC a ring, just on the off-chance that any documents have come in. I'm going to get my head down for an hour or two and then I'll come on up, OK?'

'Fine, John, leave it with me. See you in a while.'

He took the coffee to bed and lay there, one hand crooked behind his head. He didn't need to open the wardrobe or the chest of drawers.

When he woke he went to the bathroom and felt the flannels that lay over the side of the bath: they were stiff, hadn't been used for a couple of days.

He had a quick bath and changed his clothes. He tipped the contents of his holdall on to the floor in a pile on his side of the bed and rummaged in the airing cupboard for clean underwear and socks. There were a couple of clean shirts, and he took those too.

He drove north-west in a trance-like state of post-wakefulness. He had known for some time now that he and Kath would part. And he had feared it. It was a step away from the familiar. A step into the unknown.

He was waiting for the pain to begin.

He drove on, too fast, and watched his feelings closely, expecting at any moment to be smothered by gloom and sadness and hurt.

But it didn't come, and he actually found it difficult to keep at the front of his mind what was happening, and where the pain should lie.

He wound down the window and let the warm breeze play through his damp hair. He thought of the girl with the faint bruise and gawky nose and fair hair under her arm. He felt unaccountably good, and switched on the radio. Buddy Holly was singing *Peggy Sue* and he sang along with it, quietly at first, and then louder, until he was singing at the top of his voice.

He only ever felt high like this when a case was close to being solved. But this case was nowhere near a solution.

He smiled, carried on singing, and thought of the girl.

CHAPTER TWENTY-TWO

At Welshpool Police Station Rees met him in front reception and walked him straight to his waiting car.

'What's up?' said Munroe.

'We've found it,' said Rees.

'The 1100? Already?'

'The very same,' said Rees.

'Where is it, then?' asked Munroe.

'Len Hughes's yard.'

'Len Hughes?' said Munroe. 'Who's he? Where did he get it?'

'He's not saying,' said Rees.

'Not saying? What do you mean, he's not saying?'

Rees negotiated the steep bends up to Hughes's yard in his Morris Oxford. He slowed to a crawl as he took the last of the corners before the yard. The hedgerows were rampant: ox-eye daisies, succulent, green-shafted, grey-budded bluebells, speedwell, red campion and wild chamomile.

They parked in a passing place just beyond the hand-painted sign, Llanarmon Motors.

At the gate stood a uniformed sergeant who cupped his cigarette in his hand as the two men approached.

There was the sound of a radio playing in the yard and a man's feet were sticking out from beneath an old black Vauxhall Wyvern.

Dr Child was sitting on the cottage doorstep, his eyes shaded from the low afternoon sun. There was the sweet, coconut smell of gorse on the air. As the policemen approached, the doctor moved towards the inert body beneath the Vauxhall.

Munroe could tell from the man's legs that he was dead: he had assumed a writhing shape, unlike anything that belonged to the living.

'How?' said Munroe as the little doctor came towards them.

His checked green and brown suit had a comfortable, lived-in appearance, but his brogues were clean and he walked gingerly among the ruts and oily patches on the ground.

'How? Asphyxiation, I imagine. The Inspector here asked me not to move him until you'd arrived. When I got here, there was no sign of pulse. He was clearly dead. Warm day, but the man was cold. He had obviously been dead for some hours. It's not possible to say how long until we have a look at what he had for breakfast.' The country doctor appeared to be looking forward to examining the contents of the dead man's stomach.

The Inspector got down on his knees and peered beneath the car. He swallowed hard to control the spasm that rose violently from his gut to his throat as he saw the tortured expression on the dead man's face. He got up and inhaled deeply, the coconut scent drawn in until he felt heady with it.

The policemen took a few steps away from the body. 'Who found him?' said Munroe.

'Postman,' said Rees. 'Brian Jennings. He came up here with a parcel at about eleven o'clock this morning. The radio was on, and he saw Len working under the car. He gets down to tell him he's got a parcel and gets the shock of his life. He threw up in the grass over there. Then he cycled down to the village where he phoned us from the post office.'

The Beatles sang *Lady Madonna* over the scene. Munroe, affronted by the incongruity, shouted at the sergeant at the gate, 'Turn that bloody thing off, for Christ's sake.'

'Funny thing is,' continued Rees, 'as soon as I got here, it wasn't Len that I saw first, but that.' He pointed to the green Austin 1100 that was parked beside the fence.

They walked towards the car. There were mud splashes around the front wheel arches where Len had ploughed through puddles on the lane, and he'd draped an old grey blanket over the driver's seat to protect it from his greasy overalls, but there was nothing else to distinguish it in any way.

Munroe said to Rees, his fingers on the wing of the car, 'I've just driven a four-hundred-mile round trip to find this!'

Rees offered the comfort, 'If you hadn't gone to his flat, we wouldn't even have known that we were looking for it.'

'Funny though, eh?' said Munroe mirthlessly.

'Hilarious,' said the Welshman. 'What about Len? Shall we get him out now?'

'Yes, sure.'

'Poor bastard,' said Rees with feeling. 'All for the sake of an axle stand. What are they? Couple of quid from Halford's?'

There was a crow's squawk, and a loose, dry twig bounced through the branches of a tree from one of the ramshackle nests near by.

'Who was he?' asked Munroe.

'Local fixit. Bit of mechanicking, you know, work on your car for the M.O.T., that sort of thing. Not very good, but cheap.'

'Nothing else?' said Munroe, 'Any form?'

'Nothing serious. A bald tyre, no tax, that kind of thing. He was up before the local worthies a few months ago for a bit of clocking on a Mini he'd sold.'

'So what's he doing with Charlie's car here?'

'You've got me. Maybe he bought it. Perhaps the youngster needed the readies, and Len gave him them?'

'And then Charlie ends up dead? And not much more than a week later the guy who's got his car is dead too? Do you know any Hardy, Tony?'

'No, but I like the song.' He started to hum 'All Over the World'.

'Not Françoise, you berk. Thomas, the writer!'

'Only joking, John. Dylan's the only Thomas we read at school round here. Why? Is he good on suspicious deaths?'

'He always puts in just one coincidence too many: the accidental meeting; the letter that doesn't arrive; the person who walks by at just the right time to hear the crucial conversation. It makes me uneasy. And this is the same. Coincidences: definitely one too many.'

'Maybe,' said Rees, slow to acquiesce.

Policemen in overalls started to manœuvre the big trolley jack underneath the car while Munroe and Rees smoked and the doctor peered down at his corpse.

'What do *you* reckon's going on then, Tony?'

'I've no idea. This used to be a quiet spot,' the Welshman said, 'It's a good job the hippies *are* moving in if we're going to lose the locals at this rate!'

Munroe grinned. 'What about DVLC on the 1100? Any good there?'

'Nothing yet. Too soon, I should think.'

'Have you had a look inside?' said Munroe, nodding towards the cottage that abutted the workshop.

'A quick look. I can't see anything obvious. The log book's probably in the post. But what'll that tell us that we don't already know?'

'Just the day he bought it, not that that's of much use, even if he puts the exact right date on it. I'd better take a look, anyway.'

'Shall we get it up, sir?' shouted the sergeant from beside the huge black Wyvern.

'Yes, carry on,' said Rees, and the car was inched up from the man's crushed chest.

CHAPTER TWENTY-THREE

Mickey Gynn had registered in his own name at the Bear in Llanfrynach, and tracing him to his London address was a straightforward matter. A couple of Metropolitan CID men picked him up and he gave the detectives the address of his colleague, Ibrahim Malik. He, too, was detained at his house in Peckham.

The two men, isolated from one another, were driven through the night to Wales.

The next day, at Welshpool HQ, kept apart and inter-viewed separately, their stories remained identical. Charlie Somerville owed them some money; 'a loan'. They'd come up to collect it. He might have left London to avoid them. Who knows? In any event, they had come up and 'seen' him. 'Had a word', as they delicately put it. He said he was going to get the money. Said he had it in hand.

And the deep gash on Charlie's leg, asked Munroe? A gash that was very recent and not likely to have been caused by the fatal crash, according to the examining pathologist.

'I don't know nothin' about that,' said Gynn indif-ferently.

In Munroe's experience, contrary to received wisdom, you certainly *could* judge books by their covers. He was a convinced physiognomist. The thug lounging in the chair in front of him had the expressionless eyes and cruel mouth that Munroe habitually associated with a capacity to inflict pain, and a callous indifference to the feelings of others.

It was only in the pages of fiction and on the cinema and TV screens that, for novelty's sake, the kindly man and sweet-looking woman committed barbarous acts. The mur-derers and rapists that Munroe had sent down resembled, if not Rotweilers and Dobermans, at least cunning terriers and sly mongrels.

Depressingly, Rees and Munroe had no answer to the question they posed themselves: Why would these two, having used violence and intimidation against Charles, then want to kill their debtor. And, indeed, in such an absurdly contrived manner. And anyway, if they had come up here to fulfil a contract on young Somerville, they would hardly have registered at a village pub in the area, and certainly not in their own names.

The arranged meeting between Gynn and Malik and the boy the following day had never taken place. They were having a drink in the Bear that evening when they heard one of the locals relating the tragedy of the fatal accident. They checked out of the inn the next morning and returned to London empty-handed. 'Such is life,' said Gynn dismissively.

Munroe asked, 'How much did he owe you?' And before he could answer, 'Enough for two of you to come up here and cut him up? How much?'

'I got nothin' to say about that. He owed us a couple of grand. Not a fortune, but it had to be paid,' said Gynn phlegmatically.

The trouble was, it was all entirely plausible. The Met had told Montgomeryshire that Gynn and Malik were with the Maitland firm. So it was drugs-related money. But what did that mean? That Charlie dealt drugs. Maybe the boy had been stung, or rolled. But so what? That didn't assist them. Did he owe others money, too? Why would someone want him dead?

They pummelled away at them for hours, on and on, exploring all the angles, but these weren't local, small-time hoods who were going to be frightened at the sight of the town beak. They knew the score. And the score was no score.

In desperation, and with considerable professional chag-
rin, Munroe decided to wheel out to Malik the old nonsense
about Gynn having told them 'the truth', and that in his
own best interests, Malik had better now collaborate.

The six-foot-two Senegalese bared his white teeth and
laughed a huge, good-natured laugh at the two detectives
who were prepared to insult his criminal sang-froid in this
way. He said nothing and continued to smoke Pall Mall
from the red paper packet and suck the smoke from his
mouth up into his wide nostrils.

With regard to Len Hughes, they said that they'd never
heard of the man, and Munroe suspected that they were
probably telling the truth.

Later that day, as Gynn and Malik headed down to London
in an unmarked police car, the detectives returned to Plas
Trisillio.

The Colonel came out to meet them on the gravel forecourt and shook hands with each of them. Munroe offered
his condolences to the bereaved father, and Somerville
ushered them into the kitchen. 'Tea? Coffee, gentlemen?'

The Colonel pulled his cap from his sandy hair and
started to make instant coffee in three mugs.

Munroe began, 'You have probably heard that Len
Hughes was found dead yesterday?'

'Yes. One of the men told me last evening. Tragic. He
was working under a car and the thing fell on him. Is that
so?'

'Yes, it looks like it,' replied the Inspector.

'Awful,' said the Colonel. He spooned the coffee into the
mugs.

'Did you know that he had a car of your son's in his
yard, Colonel?'

'A car of Charles's?' He turned and looked at Munroe,
puzzled. 'Charles didn't have a car.'

'It seems that he bought one. The day before he left London.'

'Charles did?' replied the Colonel, 'Are you sure?'

'Yes. He drove up here in it, and we found it at Hughes's yard.'

He looked from one policeman to the other. 'But Charles told me that he had come up by train.'

'I don't think so,' said Munroe.

'Well, why should he say that? And why would he buy a car and not tell me?'

He turned and poured the boiling water on to the coffee.

'I don't know,' said Munroe. 'He certainly bought the car. And equally certainly he didn't travel by train out of London that day: the trains were on strike. Why he told you that he did is something of a mystery to us.'

'And to me,' offered the Colonel. He leaned back against the huge Welsh dresser and a couple of china serving plates rocked ominously.

'When he took your car—' Munroe paused respectfully—'the day he died ... do you have any idea where he might have been going?'

'I'm afraid not.' He reflected. 'It was unusual for him to take my car. I prefer being the only driver.' Even now, after this tragedy, there was the hint of an admonition about the comment. 'But his mother's had a puncture, and I was out in the Land-Rover, so whatever it was that he needed to do, he felt that he had to take mine, I suppose.'

'Had your car been involved in any accident at any time? Anything that might have damaged the bonnet at all?' asked Rees.

'No. Why do you ask?' said Somerville, as he placed the men's coffee in front of them on the table.

'There's a possibility that it had been tampered with. We need to make certain that the bonnet hadn't been damaged in any way before your son's accident in it,' said Munroe.

'What do you mean? Who would tamper with my car?'

'Perhaps you can help us answer that question,' said Munroe.

'I don't see how, but do go on,' said the Colonel.

'Are you sure you have no idea where your son might have been going?'

'None.'

'Do you know that your son gambled, Colonel?'

'Yes, I know he had the odd bet.'

Rees interrupted, 'He had more than the "odd bet", sir. He gambled heavily. For a young man at college he was spending a lot on horses.'

'No, I didn't know that,' said the Colonel. 'He was losing, I imagine?' He thought of his son's plea for a loan only two days before he had died.

'As a matter of fact, he was doing quite well,' said Rees.

Munroe drew from his jacket pocket a copy of the turf accountant's statement. He pushed it across to the Colonel. 'It was only recently that he seemed to have run into some difficulty.' The Inspector put his finger on the two big debits of ten days ago, 'He had a couple of big bets, and they both went down. But then, although it's not shown on this statement, he paid in two hundred and seventy-five pounds a couple of days after he arrived up here. He paid it in at the little branch in Llanfrynach. The last telephone bet that he made was on the day before his death. He staked four hundred pounds on a horse called Rhyme 'n' Reason.'

'Four hundred pounds! He bet four hundred pounds on one horse?'

'Yes. It came in at 9 to 4. Gave him credit of about thirteen hundred pounds. We understand that he owed someone about two thousand pounds.'

'Do you have any idea what for?' asked Somerville cautiously, fearing the worst.

'We can't be certain, but it very much looks as if he was involved with selling drugs.'

'I see,' he said despairingly.

'When he died, he had a piece of paper in his pocket with some figures on it. It mystified us at first, but now it seems that they were the probable odds on a horse that was running that day. He owed these characters a couple of thousand, and it seems that he was using his gambling knowledge to try and raise it. I'm afraid it all fits. Except his death.'

'You don't seem entirely surprised,' said Rees. 'Did he tell you that he needed money?'

'Yes,' said the Colonel, 'Not in so many words, but he asked me for a loan. The day he came home. He asked me if I could lend him fifteen hundred pounds.' The two men waited. The Colonel looked up. 'Naturally, I couldn't,' he said, defensively.

'And did he say why he wanted it?'

'A business deal. A "short-term business opportunity" were his exact words.' He pushed his fingers through his hair. 'But where does the car you mentioned fit in with all this?'

'We think he bought a car to get out of London quickly ... then he sold it ... to Len Hughes, so that he could get some cash, some collateral, into his bookmaker's account. He needed stake money.'

'And where was he going in mine? Where was he driving to?'

'To place his bet,' said Munroe.

'But you've just said he'd got an account. He was in credit. Why couldn't he telephone the bookmakers?'

'We think that's what he was doing.'

'What do you mean? There are phones in the house. He could have used any one of them.'

'On the contrary. The day your son died was the day after the storm. It brought down all the lines. I think he was trying to get to a phone-box that was still working.'

'I see. And the urgency? His "creditors" I suppose?'

Rees nodded agreement.

'They came up here?' said Somerville forlornly.

'Yes, we think so,' said Rees.

There was a pause while the policemen let the Colonel absorb the facts.

Eventually he said, 'Forgive me, gentlemen, but how does any of this tie in with someone tampering with *my* car?'

Munroe answered him with a question, 'When I spoke to your wife, I asked her if she knew of anyone who might want to do you any harm. Do you know of anyone with a grudge against you?'

'No, I don't think so,' he said thoughtfully.

'No one at all?' said Rees.

'No.'

'Would you think about it, and if anything occurs, give us a call? It could be important.'

'Of course,' said Somerville.

Munroe got to his feet, 'Before we leave, is your wife available for a few words, sir?'

The Colonel reached out for Rees's empty cup, 'I'm afraid my wife is in hospital. Dr Child arranges for her to spend a few days there occasionally.' He put the cups in the sink. 'She has a . . . dietary problem, you know.'

The policemen glanced at one another. This was an original euphemism. They expressed their sympathy.

'Frankly, she hasn't been coping since Charles's death,' said her husband.

'Perhaps some other time,' said Munroe.

'Of course,' said the Colonel. 'If you find anything, you will let me know?'

'Certainly,' said Munroe. 'Just before we go, your groom—' he looked at his notebook—'Susie Peterson, and her friend—James, James Orme, the young couple from Well Cottage. How well do you know them?'

There was a little hesitation before the Colonel replied, 'She's very good with the horses. Excellent, in fact.'

'What about the boy?' said Munroe, 'Have you ever had anything to do with him? They've split up recently.'

'No, nothing. I've never spoken to him. I saw him working with Hopkins from Pentre farm once, passed them on the lane once or twice, that's all.'

The three men walked along the corridor to the front door. On the drive the Colonel put on his tweed cap and stood waiting. The terrier sniffed at the gravel.

Rees got into the car, but Munroe walked a few yards towards the rhododendron bushes; the Colonel followed him. The Inspector looked at the tight buds at the ends of the leathery green leaves. He spoke very slowly and deliberately, 'Colonel Somerville, your son has died. It looks like murder. I think that you may well have been the intended victim. I think that you owe it to your son's memory to be honest with me.'

'What are you talking about?' said the Colonel. 'Be honest with you about what?'

'You said you knew of no one who would wish to hurt you. In my experience, the husbands of women who are having affairs tend to want to hurt their rivals.'

'Fry!' said Somerville derisively. 'Good God! Heaven preserve us from policemen. Do you ever solve anything?'

His indignation was genuine and Munroe faltered, 'What do you mean? Are you telling me that George Fry doesn't know about his wife and you?'

'Of course he *knows*. He knows and he's perfectly happy. He has his own . . . "interests".'

'Go on,' said Munroe.

'The man's a solicitor. In and out of court, dinner with JPs, even the Lord Lieutenant of Shropshire now and again. He can't turn up at functions and cocktail parties with his *boy*friends! Nicola is his appendage. He keeps her well, doesn't interfere with her life; she's discreet and sits through Rotary dinners and Town-twinning lunches. It's an *arranged* marriage, Inspector. And the arrangement works very well. The idea that George Fry is going to bugger it up (you'll forgive the phrase) by interfering with me is, frankly, absurd.'

Munroe felt extremely stupid. He shuffled to the car and, as he stepped in, said bitterly, 'Give my regards to Mrs Somerville.'

'That was a bit severe, wasn't it?' said Rees, as they drove away.

'Yes,' said Munroe.

CHAPTER TWENTY-FOUR

A mile and a half by the twisted lane, five hundred yards as the crows flew between Plas Trisillio's beechwood and Pentrefelin Hill, Munroe and Rees made their way up to Well Cottage.

Rees was about to get out of the car when Munroe put his hand on the other man's elbow. 'Tony, do you think it might be better if just one of us spoke to them at first? You know, burly cops and all.'

'No,' said Rees, 'I don't.' He winked at Munroe, 'But good luck!'

The cottage door was open and the choral movement of Beethoven's Ninth Symphony filled all the little house and garden. The girl was singing along with it. He knocked, put his head into the room and called, 'Hello.'

She came from the kitchen and turned the music down. Her legs were brown in a short skirt of blue velvet, her feet were bare and she had painted nails, which his mother had once assured him only harlots and film stars wore.

'Hello again,' she said, warmly, 'come in. Would you like some tea, I've got the kettle on?'

He sat in the armchair as she made the tea and the music reached its demented crescendo. On her chair was a well-read copy of *Sons and Lovers*. There were several pictures on the wall, mostly watercolour landscapes, and pretty bunches of wild flowers on the table and the mantelpiece.

When the music stopped she came in and said, 'Shall we have something different?' She knelt down to the stereo and her little skirt rode up to her thighs. Her brown legs had downy, fair hair that she obviously didn't shave. It looked lovely and soft, he thought.

As she went back into the kitchen Bob Dylan began to sing. It was 'Freewheelin''. He had often heard Kath play it and he felt a hypocrite as he called, rather proudly, 'I've got this, too.'

'It's James's. One of his he didn't take,' she replied from the kitchen.

She brought in the tray with a pot of tea and nice blue and white teacups with matching saucers. 'Honey?'

'Do you have any sugar?' he asked.

She went back to the kitchen and returned with some gloomy-looking sugar in a teak bowl.

'Are you reading this?' He held her battered Penguin in his hand.

'Yes. It's my favourite novel. I've read it once every year since school. Do you like it?'

He felt the colour rising in his neck. Kath had introduced him to what she called 'proper' books. And very many of the authors that she had helped him discover, he loved. He probably read more poetry than she did now, found that he could read a poem or two, whereas it was often difficult finding the time to get through a chapter of a novel. But he had started his education late, and read slowly and carefully; he had huge gaps. He had never read any D. H. Lawrence. 'I haven't read much by him,' he muttered.

'I'm sure you'd love it,' she said.

He was charmed that she made no attempt to expose his obvious lie.

She looked up at him, 'He knows so much. And when he's writing at his peak, he's like a man possessed.'

Munroe began to feel threatened by the bearded writer. 'Yes, I'd like to read it,' he said sincerely.

She went to the kitchen for milk and lemon.

He found it easier when she wasn't beside him, 'Has James . . . ?' he called.

She didn't help him.

'Your friend . . . James . . . he's gone somewhere . . . ?'

She walked back in. 'Yes, he's gone,' she said inconclusively.

'I was hoping to speak to him. When did he leave?'

'A couple of days ago.' She sat on the floor facing him, her legs tucked under her, and poured the tea. 'Things haven't been very good between us. When we got out of London, it was all right for a while, and then there was some awful business with the farmer up the hill.' She related the story of the farmer's voyeurism. 'It seemed to eat away at James. He quit the job, of course, so we had very little money, only the dole.' She looked up at him, 'You won't tell anyone this, will you?'

'Of course not,' he said.

'We came back from the village a couple of days later, and there was an envelope wedged in the door jamb. It had some money in it. What the farmer owed James, and another twenty pounds.'

'He was buying your silence?'

'I suppose so. James wouldn't have told anyone, anyway. I suppose he was afraid of his wife finding out. We like Glenys. We wouldn't have told her something like that, just to hurt her.'

'Neither of you?' probed Munroe.

'Neither of us,' she said.

'Then what?'

'Things just started to fall apart. He's jealous. I'm cramped. It's worse than London. And we've almost no money as well. When I saw the job at Plas Trisillio, I'd have done it without pay, just to get out of the cottage for a few hours each day.'

'I see,' he said. Every time that she glanced away he

looked to her thin, brown arms and nice bra-less bosom beneath her pink T-shirt.

'The job at Plas Trisillio just made things worse. He couldn't bear me being out of his sight.'

Dylan sang plaintively of 'The Girl from the North Country'.

'Eventually, we just couldn't carry on. We tried to talk it out. But in the end we decided to try being apart for a while.'

'Where's he gone?'

'To the Channel Islands. To Guernsey.'

He sat forward, 'Listen, Susie.' He thrilled to say her name, and she smiled slightly, knowing this, even though what he was saying was grave. 'James was jealous, right? First the farmer, then the Colonel. And wasn't there something in the pub when he got into a fight?'

'Yes, there was. He hit a local boy, a boy from the village. I don't even know why. He was getting impossible.'

'So what about the Colonel's car? Charles's death? You've heard the rumours, surely?'

'Yes,' she said.

'Do you think he might have tried to hurt the Colonel . . . if he thought there was something going on between you and him?'

'Look . . . Inspector Munroe.' She dwelt on the two syllables and felt rather silly calling him this, especially with his nice brown eyes taking her womanness in, 'Did you ever meet James? His idea of a crime is buying the *Daily Telegraph*. He was jealous, and I tried to reassure him. He may not have been convinced. He was insecure about us. But *we* are the people who sit in Trafalgar Square protesting about Vietnam. We don't kill people.'

She went to the table and got her cigarette tobacco. 'I know he had a temper when he was jealous. He hit me, just because that farmer had watched me.'

'Yes,' said Munroe. He lifted his finger to his own cheek at the place where the bruise had been on hers. 'I remember.'

'But he couldn't have been involved with the Colonel's car. I would have known. I'd have been able to tell.'

'How can you be so sure?'

'I just *know*,' she said. She met his eyes and they looked at one another for as long as either of them could bear.

Dylan sang, 'Where the winds hit heavy on the border line . . .' The words were affecting. He had never heard them before. Not really heard them. Sitting here with her, he no longer heard the whining voice that he had moaned to Kath about, that he had foolishly mocked.

'He *had* done something, though,' she said. 'I don't know what it was. He wouldn't tell me. He took a trip, you know, an acid trip. It was a stupid thing to do.

'He'd taken it in the morning, while I was at work at Plas Trisillio, and when I came home he was in the corner there, all folded up. I comforted him. I just held him very close.

'In the evening, as he started to come down, he told me that he'd done something bad. But he wouldn't tell me what. He said I'd never forgive him.'

'Why didn't you make him tell you?'

'Have you ever taken LSD?' she asked considerately, but certain of his answer.

'Yes, we take it as part of basic training!'

She indulged his sarcasm. 'People are on the edge, push them and they might go over. It's happened to friends of mine. It *is* a dangerous drug and it *may* be stupid to play around with it. But it can also be the most enlightening experience that most of us will ever have.'

Her obvious sincerity neutralized his Pavlovian response. He listened.

'If you're going to take it, or be with people who have

taken it, you need to be very careful. The last thing I would do would be to push James to tell me something that was causing him this much distress.'

'And afterwards? The days after. What did he tell you then?'

'He wouldn't tell me anything. He said it was just a bad trip.'

The policeman's instinct returned with a crude vengeance. 'Great. The man's there and he's about to tell you. Don't you see? He wants to *confess* to the killing.'

'I don't believe it,' she interrupted.

'It's obvious. He tried to kill the Colonel in a fit of paranoid jealousy, and he killed his son instead.' He put his thumb and forefinger together, 'And he got that close to telling you.'

'I don't believe it,' she said again. 'I know James. If he'd done it, I would have known, and if I'd known I would have gone to the police.'

'Would you?' he said instantly. And then conciliatory, 'Are you sure?'

'No, I'm *not* sure,' she said. 'But I *think* I would.'

The song ended and she turned down the volume after the first few words of the strident 'Masters of War'.

He looked at her. She looked chagrined, as if her faith in her former lover had been shaken a little.

'I'll have to go and see him,' he said. 'I've got to talk to him.'

'Yes,' she replied, dispirited.

'Do you have his address?'

She jotted it on a bit of paper and handed it to him.

The record went round, but there was only a faint tinniness. Between them there was silence. Neither of them knew where to look. The record eventually stopped and the gap of their silence lengthened.

He lacked courage. 'I'd better go,' he said very quietly.

She didn't respond, and they both sat there, avoiding each other's eyes. He watched the little muscle in her brown forearm twitch and pulse. He wanted to reach out and lay two fingers on it, but he only pushed his toes harder against the sole of his shoes.

What was happening? His mind was spinning. He seemed capable of anything, and yet inert, as if he might slip from his chair to the floor. He wanted this woman with a deeper yearning than he had felt since he was sixteen. And yet his wanting wasn't that deep lust and urgent animal passion of teenage. He wanted to touch her ankles and wiry arms, kiss tenderly her breasts, hold her close to him, kiss her neck and nose and forehead and eyelids.

What was happening? He was a cop from Birmingham who liked a beer and to watch the football on TV. The woman kneeling in front of him smoked cannabis, had all Bob Dylan's records and painted her toenails bright red.

'Perhaps I could borrow one of Dylan's other LPs sometime?' He felt absolutely mortified as he heard himself saying the fey words.

She smiled slightly, her lips parting.

At the door, they shook hands, a nervous, barely touching little brush, as if all their fingers had electricity in them.

Rees was lounging against the car. Munroe joined him. He was smiling.

'He wasn't there, then?' said the Welshman gauchely.

Munroe said nothing.

Rees turned the car round and started down the lane.

She was standing at the cottage gate. He stopped. She passed a record in through the open window.

CHAPTER TWENTY-FIVE

When they got back to the station, the desk sergeant pointed to the woman sitting in reception who had been waiting for them for over an hour.

A couple of poachers were making their feeble excuses in the interview room on the ground floor and so the two detectives led the woman up the stairs and into the chaotic incident room with its phones and files and crisp packets and coffee cups with rings on them. Rees called for some tea.

She looked tired and rather grubby. Her dark hair was lank and greasy, her complexion oily. She was wearing purple slacks with elastic at the bottom of them that held them tight around the soles of her feet, and cheap white shoes with a little heel. Her cream jumper rode up her midriff and there was a faint stain on the big, shapeless chest.

She sat across from Rees. Munroe propped himself up in the corner of the room. Behind her was one of the blackboards that was being used on the Somerville and Hughes cases and which was covered in a smudgy maze of lines and dates and times.

'Billy killed him,' she began. 'It was an accident. He sold us the car. I told him we couldn't afford it, but he said it'd be all right. He scraped everything together, he even sold his old bike. It cost us a hundred and thirty pounds.'

Rees made no attempt to get any of it down. When the constable barged open the door and brought in the tea, he gave him a nod and pointed to the chair by the door. The youth sat quietly and listened, and was finally glad that he had joined the police force rather than gone into the Forestry Commission.

She carried on. The words came tumbling, without thought. 'There was nothing but trouble with it. He hadn't done the work that he'd promised Billy he'd do before we had it. He said he'd make it all right, but he didn't. He went back to Hughes, and they had a row, a big one. But it was an accident. Billy would never do anything like that. We've got children.

'I told him: "We've got to tell the truth. Tell the truth and they'll believe you. We can't live with something like this." You will believe him, won't you?' she pleaded.

'I'm sure you've done the right thing,' said Rees, without hope.

She started again, 'When he came back that day, I knew something was wrong. He wouldn't say what had happened. He went to the pub that night, but didn't eat all day. He got drunk, and fell asleep. When I woke up it was three o'clock in the morning and he wasn't there. I went downstairs and he was sitting in the dark, crying. I made him tell me.'

'Where is he now?' asked Rees, quietly.

'At home, with the children. He's waiting. You will believe him won't you?' she said again.

Her husband was just as she had suggested: a small man, who was cowed by the world in general and now by his monstrous crime in particular. He wanted to oblige: as Rees interviewed him, he tried to complete the end of the detective's sentences with him, mouthing the last few words as they drew to a close.

He smoked constantly, rolling thin cigarettes from a battered Old Holborn tin, the first two fingers of his right hand shiny nut-brown from the years of nicotine.

He filled in the details. He'd gone back for the fourth

time. The clutch was slipping. It was the last straw. Hughes had been dismissive. 'What do you want for a hundred quid?' he had said.

'I want a car that goes for longer than a week,' said Williams.

He made some half-hearted threats about legal action, but Hughes had laughed them off.

'Get off my land,' said the mechanic. 'I've work to do. Go on, get off.'

He had slid under the Wyvern and seen the man's footsteps disappear. Hughes had the bleed spanner on the brake nipple.

Williams, twenty yards away, was coming to the boil. Hughes was a powerfully built man, altogether bigger and stronger than him. But not at this moment. The man exploded with the rage of years. Every injustice that he had ever felt was pent in the kick that he lashed out at the pile of bricks. The Vauxhall rocked for a moment before it collapsed on the prone mechanic.

Then, said Williams, he had begun his heroic struggle. He tried to lift the car from on top of the dying man.

Whether this was true or not was hardly material. His 'brief' would have invented it for his defence anyway, 'mitigating circumstances'. What *was* true was that this small, frightened man with a tattoo saying 'Sylvia' on his forearm had killed another. He had panicked. Was scared stiff by what he had accidentally done, and so had driven away.

His wife had eventually made him come and tell the truth. She said that it would be all right, that he would be believed. He *would* be believed, wouldn't he? He started to cry uncontrollably.

Rees pushed his packet of cigarettes towards the man.

With a sympathetic jury, if he got a haircut, had his wedding suit cleaned, and got a decent lawyer to take an interest for the price of a legal aid fee, he might be out of Winson Green in five or six years.

'Yes, you'll be all right. Don't worry,' said Rees despondently. 'You'll be fine.'

CHAPTER TWENTY-SIX

That night, in the pitch black of his room in the White Horse in Welshpool, Munroe found it impossible to sleep. In the darkness, he fingered his chin against the growth and knew from the stubble that it was only four or five o'clock. He lay there and sweated. Even thoughts of the girl at the cottage could not divert him from his anxiety.

He loathed the prospect of flying. If asked to put next month's salary, or even his mortgage, on whether the Viscount would crash or not, he knew that his money would be secure, invested in the safe landing of the aeroplane. But his was an irrational fear: the engines that screamed at an apparently unsustainable pitch; the ambling, yawing of the huge, ungainly structure, its aluminium shell stuffed full of wiring and brimming to its dangerous gills with high-octane fuel. The way it lumbered down the tarmac and how, at the end of the runway, the captain seemed to jest with the mortals strapped in their seats as he tested the spongy brakes.

And then, the gut-wrenching moment of ascent, the parting of the huge, spinning tyres from the tarmac, the absolute letting go, the point of no return as the passengers became literally suspended between life and death.

Munroe was well aware that an anxiety about allowing your fate to be in the hands of others was a basic manifestation of insecurity. He had read all about it. But so what? Knowing *that* didn't help. It was like a condemned man being expected to draw solace from his understanding of gallows technology.

For he also knew that this plane, hurtling through thin air at hundreds of miles an hour, had had its oil topped up, and its bolts tightened, and its wiring checked by men exactly like the ones at his local garage who left the top off the engine-oil filler in his car, connected the spark plug leads in the wrong order, and never inflated tyres to the correct pressure. They, too, had rows with their wives, had too much to drink at the club or pub, and lost a mother or a favourite dog. But they still came to work and tightened the bolts and checked the wires and topped up the oil on the plane.

In Munroe's view, aeroplane maintenance should be undertaken only by celibates, men who spent their rest days and weekends in prayer and quiet contemplation.

The flight from Birmingham's Elmdon airport to Guernsey was not until two in the afternoon, and Munroe had left himself plenty of time to call at the hospital in Shrewsbury on his way down to the Midlands to speak to Dorothea Somerville and her therapist.

At reception he was directed to the doctor's room by a young lady whose moving lips he watched closely. When she had finished gesturing each right and left turn in the corridors with the 2B pencil in her hand, Munroe knew that she was left-handed, bit her nails, smoked (holding the cigarette in her right hand), and that she had a double filling in her lower left jaw. Unfortunately, he still had absolutely no idea where Dr Pickering's room was. He thanked her and, continuing to watch her, walked hesitantly away down the corridor, gesturing vaguely ahead of him, hoping that she might either confirm or contradict his route for as long as he had sight of her.

Nigel Pickering, consultant psychiatrist at Shelton Hospital, was a well-intentioned, kindly man who gave generously to charity, pushed hospital beds around the centre of the town to raise money for the new wing, and was an excellent father. When he had read bedtime stories to his children, Nathan and Iphigenia, he had made the noises, pulled the faces, grimaced the grimaces and even cried the tears.

When they were older, the family, in all weathers, walked Offa's Dyke, the Pembrokeshire Coastal Path and the Pennine Way. The Pickerings observed other holidaying families with a sort of benign dismay as they ate ice-cream and squabbled in the back of Ford Escorts.

By the time that they were at the local state grammar school, and their chums were going on sudden excursions to Majorca or the Costa Del Sol, Nathan and Iphigenia were accompanying their parents to the Austrian Tyrol and the Italian lakes, where the air was clean and the lakes were not full of people with Dudley accents who piddled in the water.

On their alpine holidays, Dr Pickering eulogized the flowers and the clouds and the birds. Any that he did not know he looked up in one of the little books that he carried in his canvas knapsack, along with interesting articles from *Psychiatry Today* and a selection of crosswords that he had collected from the *Observer* during the month preceding the holiday.

Nathan and Iphigenia emerged from adolescence as emotionally stunted children whose capacity to respond directly to almost anything had been effectively nullified by their over-zealous father. The good, liberal psychiatrist, who had devoted his career to helping the mentally ill, and whom his children had once heard wax lyrical about a pile of sheep droppings on the alpine pastures, had virtually appropriated their capacity to feel. They never forgave him.

At work in the hospital, even in a profession which dealt daily with the deranged, the deluded and the mad, his

ability to get under the skin of both those in his care, and
his peers, was nothing short of remarkable.

As Munroe sat in the psychiatrist's room opposite the
robustly healthy, prematurely balding man, he felt an inde-
finable antipathy towards him: what *was* it about a man's
eating an apple in public that sought to confer upon him
such moral superiority, he wondered?

Dorothea Somerville had been in the hospital several times
during the last three or four years. He could get her file
and tell the Inspector the precise dates, 'if you so wish' (the
implication was that he would not be going to do this). She
exhibited many of the traits and symptoms of the middle-
aged, female alcoholic: a husband who no longer appeared
interested in her; children growing up and leading more or
less independent lives; essentially, an overwhelming sense
of her own innate worthlessness.

On her admission to Pickering's unit, the process now
followed an established routine: withdrawal from all alcohol, regular intake of vitamin B supplements, and a course
of Nembutal, which helped to combat her anxiety and produced the drowsiness and detachment that allowed her
some fitful sleep. When ready, she would join the psycho-
therapy group, and would rehearse her problems under the
careful guidance of 'my good self'.

'Unfortunately,' he continued, 'once out of the hospital
environment, she will no doubt begin again the steady
drinking that will eventually lead to her re-admission in a
few months' time.' The doctor twirled his apple core by its
stalk between his thumb and finger. 'Very sad. Very tragic,'
he said thoughtfully.

'There's no chance of her giving up her drinking?' asked
Munroe.

'None whatsoever,' said the doctor emphatically. 'There
are many treatments for alcoholism, Inspector Munroe, but

there is one absolute requirement: the patient has to want to stop. Mrs Somerville has never expressed any real wish to do so.'

'I see,' said Munroe, feeling rather chastened by the doctor's use of his name and rank, as if *he* were in some way responsible for Mrs Somerville's malaise. He patted his jacket pocket and took out his cigarettes. Pickering immediately went to the french windows of his room and pushed them open.

'And at what stage is her treatment at the moment?' asked Munroe as he lit a Gold Leaf.

'She's still in detoxification,' said the doctor, emphasizing the word and theatrically averting his face from Munroe's cigarette smoke. 'She'll be feeling groggy for a while. Is it about her son's death?'

'Yes,' said Munroe. 'You obviously know about it?'

'Of course,' said the doctor.

'I have to ask her a few questions. But it's not urgent. It'll keep.'

'She won't be much help to you for a day or two yet, I'm afraid,' said the doctor.

'Thank you,' said Munroe, getting to his feet. 'I'll call back, then. May I go out this way? I've got a bit of time to kill. Perhaps I could walk round the field?'

'Certainly,' said the doctor, 'Be my guest.' As the two men stood at the french windows Pickering drew back his arm and threw his apple core as far as he could into the field. Munroe looked at him, a little surprised. 'Bio-degradable,' said the doctor, 'bio-degradable.'

'I see,' said Munroe. To his eyes it looked like a half-eaten apple core on a nicely mown cricket field.

CHAPTER TWENTY-SEVEN

Detective-Inspector Lefebvre met Munroe at Guernsey airport. The man looked like a prop forward, and thereafter Munroe always associated his formidable stature with the low Channel Islands crime rate. His appearance belied his good nature: he displayed none of the tiresome inter-force rivalry that plagued the mainland divisions.

He naturally wanted to know what the young man, James Orme, had done that could warrant bringing an Inspector all the way from Wales. Munroe bluffed, told him it was routine, related to an accidental death. The Channel Islands policeman was quietly unimpressed with this baloney and told his wife at supper that evening that he believed the Inspector with the Birmingham accent was probably here to detain a murder suspect.

He drove Munroe up the steep road that looked down to the harbour where the boy had taken lodgings with a jewellery retailer's widow.

Les Vardes was a boxy, flat-roofed building that was cleverly designed on two levels to tuck neatly into the contours of the hillside. Covered in glistening white stucco it needed repainting every two years as it took the buffeting of the Atlantic winter storms before they blew down to the gulf of St Malo thirty miles away.

Lefebvre sat in the driver's seat of the Peugeot, with the door open, and smoked Gitanes while Munroe went up to the garden. The ornamental bushes were pruned, the flowerbeds weeded and mulched and the hedges neatly clipped. The brass door-pull and handle shone and the timber plaque upon which the name of the house was mounted was worn smooth by years of polishing. Even the gravel on the path looked clean.

As he stood in the warm sun at the door a tortoiseshell cat came up to him and arched its back against his calf.

Mrs Sandy, crippled by arthritis, led him into the kitchen. She confirmed that she had taken the young man as a lodger, and explained to the Inspector that she liked to feel the presence of someone else in the house. He had replied to her advert in the *Guernsey Chronicle*. On the telephone he had sounded very nice. But when he had walked through the wrought-iron gate an hour later and she saw his long hair, she had been ready to lie to him and tell him that the rooms had been let.

It was not that she was afraid of him: more than twenty-five years ago, German officers had stood on her balcony and surveyed the harbour approaches. It would take more than a long-haired boy in blue jeans to frighten her. But she really didn't care for the hippies that visited the island in greater numbers every year now, looking for work in the tomato-packing warehouses or picking flowers in the huge commercial greenhouses or serving ice-cream in the beach cafés. They did the work, but there was also talk of drugs, and they busked in the square and many of the tourists didn't like them and their dirty looks. They were a mixed blessing.

But by the time that she had been ready to explain to him that she could no longer let the room, he had won her over. His hair might have been down to his shoulders but he was courteous and polite. He talked to her about her illness, seemed to know quite a lot about the different forms of it, said his grandmother was also incapacitated through it. She castigated herself for being such an old fuddy-duddy, told herself that it was the beginning of the end when you started looking inward and rejected everything that was new.

She had showed him the room and they had agreed the terms there and then.

The boy was out at work, driving Turner's mineral water lorry. He would be back at about five, she told the Inspector. Mrs Sandy wanted to know what he had done, but he told her only that he needed to speak to the boy.

They heard the gate open and then the heavy front door. The boy came into the kitchen. He was wearing jeans and plimsolls and a T-shirt. He had already caught the sun and started to tan. He looked well.

When Munroe said that he was a policeman, the boy showed no real surprise. They went up to his room on the first floor. It was tidy. There were clothes hung on hangers on the back of the door; a new Dansette portable record-player sat on a low rattan table, some books and a pile of long-playing records were stacked next to it.

The boy sat on the bed, the Inspector in the low wicker chair. 'So, what do you want with me?' he asked.

'It's about Charles Somerville. About his death. The "accident".' He drew the word out long and mocked the notion of it as he said it. 'We've got a few queries. We thought you might be able to help.'

'Susie,' he said derisively.

He ignored the boy. 'The fact is, the boy dies a mysterious death, and you leave the village a few days later. It looks suspicious. And there are other things, things that you and I both know.'

'Oh yes, "you and I",' said the boy, sneering. 'Such as?'

'Such as the problem that you have with your emotions,' said Munroe.

'I told you it was Susie. I'm disappointed in her. Very disappointed.' His supercilious tone was offensive to the policeman.

'She told me about the farmer; then there was the stuff

in the pub with one of the locals. And what about where she worked? Did you think there was something going on there?'

Orme was silent.

Munroe softened his tone. 'You're going to have to tell me, you know. It's got to be sorted out; the boy was killed. We know it was no accident.'

James took the easy bait, 'Why should I want to kill him?' he said disingenuously.

'Come on, do me a favour. *We're* from Birmingham. So people think we're stupid. The accent. But we know better, don't we? We're not *that* dim. Charlie Somerville wasn't supposed to be the victim. Even the rumours would have told you that. It was the old man. The old man . . . who's got a bit of a reputation. And you and Susie, you were going through a bad patch. She gets a job there. Come on, what next?'

'I didn't do anything,' he said.

'It won't do, James. It won't do at all. I *know* you had something on your mind.'

'Do you?'

'Yes, I do.'

'And how the fuck do you know that? 'Cause she told you, right?'

'She's been questioned. She's got to tell the truth. It's not her fault. She had to tell me what she knew.'

'So what did she tell you?'

'She told me . . . that you had things on your mind. Things that you weren't happy about. That you'd done. Maybe it would be best if you told me in your own words.'

He was not stupid. 'She didn't tell you anything, did she?'

Munroe didn't answer. 'If you've nothing to hide, why not tell me what happened? Between you and her, and the other things?'

'I did do something. I did something so shitty that I'm ashamed.'

'Yes?'

'I don't want to tell you. Or anybody else. And why should I?'

Munroe paused, looked at him and smiled, 'Because until you convince me otherwise, you're my number one suspect.'

'You're joking!' said the boy.

'I don't think so,' said Munroe seriously. 'But I'll help you if I can, I'm on your side.'

'Like fuck you are,' said the boy and he swung down from the bed and went to the kitchenette. He poured himself a tonic water and gulped it down.

Out of sight of Munroe he began in a voice that he tried to make strong, 'I did think there might have been something going on between her and Somerville.' And then, troubled, 'I still don't know whether there was . . . when I asked her, she denied it.'

'Yes,' said Munroe gently.

He deepened his voice, 'I wanted to warn him off. Warn him, and tell him how much I loved her. Loved all of her.'

'Yes?'

'I got one of her Tampax.' Munroe could hear him breathing, gasping to say the words. 'I sent it to him.'

There was an uncomfortable silence, the two men out of sight of one another. Munroe eventually said, 'A used one?'

'Yes, for Christ's sake,' he said angrily. 'What do you think I'm saying? A *used* one. Her blood on it. Herself. I wanted to disgust him, and her.'

Munroe lit a cigarette and the smoke plumed across the sun-slatted room.

The boy's disembodied voice came again, 'I was *going* to tell her what I'd done. To show her how I felt. But then I couldn't. I was afraid of what she'd do. It got more and more grotesque after I'd done it, and I couldn't tell her.

And I still don't know the truth. You've got to have truth. That's what the acid shows you. You've got to tell the truth. And I didn't, and maybe she didn't and that's why it's all gone wrong.'

He stopped gushing and there was only the silence and the blue cigarette smoke in the room and the sun and dust motes slanting through the blinds.

'You happy now?' he said pathetically, still out of sight in the kitchen. 'You can't get much lower than that, eh?'

'I don't know what to say,' said Munroe. 'And you didn't touch the car? You were prepared to do . . . that thing, but you're telling me you didn't interfere with the car?'

The boy stepped forward into the kitchen doorway, 'No, of course not.'

'How do I know you're telling me the truth?'

'You don't. What did *she* say when you asked her? Does *she* think I did it?'

'No, she doesn't,' offered Munroe. He immediately tempered the consolation with, 'But *she* could be wrong.'

Orme's confession had been cathartic. He felt some relief, some lifting of the oppression of his guilt. 'Do you want a drink?' he asked the policeman.

'Yes, please,' said Munroe.

'What do you want?'

'What have you got?'

'Orangeade, lemonade, cherryade, American cream soda, ginger beer, dandelion and burdock.'

Munroe was glad to smile. 'Dandelion and burdock, please.'

The boy poured the pop and handed it to him. 'Perks of the job,' he said, and sat on the edge of the bed again.

Munroe sipped the first dandelion and burdock he'd had in twenty years. It was exactly as he remembered it. Only now it tasted awful.

'So what happened?' said Munroe.

'What about?'

'You know, the er . . .'

'I don't know. Nothing happened. He must've got the message. He didn't say anything to Susie. Or if he did, she never told me.'

A lazy wasp battered itself against the window. Orme walked over, picked up a paper and squashed it against the glass.

Munroe believed him. He got to his feet and handed him the half-full glass. 'Are you staying here?'

'Where?'

'On the island.'

'Sure. Why?'

'At this house? And in your job?'

'Yes, I'm not going anywhere.'

'I'll need to know where you are. I'll make arrangements for you to report to the police every day. It's the best I can do. I could take you back to the mainland.'

'I'll be good, don't worry.'

They walked to the top of the stairs. 'I'll make the arrangements and the island police'll get in touch with you. And you'd better not contact anyone who's involved with the case for the time being. No letters to—'

'Susie,' he interrupted.

CHAPTER TWENTY-EIGHT

The next day Rees and Munroe used the White Horse in Welshpool for their debriefing session. They chewed over Billy Williams's confession, and Munroe filled Rees in on his day trip to Guernsey and Orme's gross gesture with the sanitary wear.

Billy Williams was exactly what a policeman doesn't want: a pathetic creature who makes one terrible mistake and spends the rest of his life paying for it. Both Rees and Munroe knew that 'real' criminals got away with murder, sometimes literally, and yet this poor bugger was going to get himself sent down for six or seven years for doing away with a nasty little rat who no one had a good word for.

But the bit that grated was the way Williams had just walked in and given himself up. They had been nowhere with the Len Hughes killing, when in steps Billy with his hands up.

They had been thrown, of course, by Charlie Somerville's car being there. The classic mistake of putting two bits of a story together that seem to fit, and yet, finally, have no connection: Len Hughes had no more to do with Charlie than buying his car; his subsequent death was a purely local affair, no more, no less. Munroe should have known better. He went to the bar and bought another round.

James Orme, Munroe felt, was innocent. His confession about the Tampax had been bitter and genuine. He was not trading a sop to them. Munroe felt that the extent of the long-haired boy's crime was this bit of perverse malice. He might be wrong, and the youth had to be watched, but he thought he was out of the frame.

But there were questions, things that didn't fit, or didn't

fit quite right: why hadn't Somerville said anything about
the Tampax? Was he simply too embarrassed? Or had
there, as Orme suspected, been something going on
between the Colonel and the girl?

Munroe seemed sure there had not. Rees gave his friend
a knowing look. So why had Somerville not mentioned this
deed, they wondered? They would go and see him again,
later this afternoon; and they would speak to the de-
toxifying Dorothea Somerville soon, perhaps tomorrow,
depending upon the advice of Dr Pickering.

Back at the station, there was a message for Rees. The desk
sergeant said Somerville had been on the phone for him.
It was nothing urgent. He would call back.

'Maybe he's going to do you for insubordination,' joked
the Welshman to his Birmingham colleague.

The two men went through to the incident room and
Rees dialled Plas Trisillio. As soon as he got through and
heard the Colonel's rounded vowels, the hint of lunch-time
insobriety disappeared and he straightened up.

'Colonel . . . DI Rees here, I got your message . . . Yes
. . . yes . . . of course . . . not at all . . . it might be useful.
No, it could be important. Let me just get it down in my
notebook . . . Yes . . . I know him . . .'

Rees gestured to the other hand-set and Munroe lifted it
carefully to his ear.

'Please, Colonel, go on.'

'It was nothing. Nothing at all. But you did say . . .'

Rees raised his eyebrows to Munroe.

'Yes, Colonel, we *did* say . . .'

Somerville continued, 'I was naturally irate. She's little
more than a child. I gave him a flea in his ear and saw
him off. I suppose he might have *some* sort of grudge. Only
God knows what I'm supposed to do when I come out and

find him in the barn with my daughter. Ask him in for a whisky and soda?'

'Quite,' said Rees. He'd noticed that people like the Colonel said 'quite' when they had nothing much to add. 'I think we'd better have a word with him. We'll get down to see him as soon as possible. And as soon as we know anything, we'll get back to you, all right?'

'Fine. I'm sure it's nothing. But you did say . . .'

'Yes, Colonel, we *did* say. Just one thing, sir, before you go.' He looked across at Munroe and the other man nodded his agreement. 'We've been speaking to the boy from Well Cottage, you know, your groom's boyfriend, James Orme.'

'Yes,' he said.

'He says he sent you something.' Rees balked at describing the item, 'Something in the post . . .'

'Yes?' said Somerville.

'Did you receive anything . . . ?'

'What do you mean? *What* did he send? When?'

'Have you received *anything* from him, Colonel?'

'Look, what's all this about? I don't know the boy. Why would he be sending anything to me?'

'Don't worry, sir, he's probably making it up. Just some story.' He looked across at Munroe who shrugged and gestured to him to put the phone down. 'We'll look into it and see what he's up to. Don't worry about it.'

'If you say so,' said the Colonel, rather testily, and Rees hung up.

'So?' said Munroe.

'You heard most of it. The usual stuff, he didn't think it was important . . . but maybe he'd better mention it, etc. The night before his boy died, he hears something in the barn, stalks over, and there's his lass with a lad from the village having a bit of nooky, you know.'

'I know,' said Munroe. 'Go on.'

'That's it. He shunts the low-life off the estate and bawls the daughter out.'

'Sounds all right to me,' said Munroe. 'People have killed for less. So who's the kid?'

'Pete Ryan. He's been in a bit of trouble, but he's all right. Bloody good player. Centre-forward for the village. Good in the air. Jumps like a salmon, hangs there and then powers it in. They say West Brom are interested in him.'

'Oh yes,' said Munroe, deeply unimpressed. Villa were his team, West Brom the local enemy. They were, in his view, just the sort of club who'd sign a murderer.

'There'll be a riot round here if he's involved,' continued Rees. 'He's got the ball control of Georgie Best.'

'If he's involved, he'll have lots of time to work on his ball skills,' said Munroe sardonically.

'Not the same inside though, is it?' said Rees regretfully.

He was big for his age, seventeen and good-looking, with blond hair down to his collar. He exuded youth and health and a certain cocky assuredness.

His mother and younger brother were in the noisy house and the policeman asked him outside for a chat. He loped towards the car, and both men felt creaky and old beside him. If he had bounded away, they knew they would never have been able to catch him.

Munroe sat in the passenger front seat and Rees shared the back with the boy. They asked a few open-ended questions to get his measure.

He didn't deny that he'd been with the girl on the night in question. And yes, the crusty father had run him off the estate.

'We'd got half our gear off . . . bloody right state we were in . . . but not as bad as him! He went ape-shit. What's he think we do at night? Go to the village hall for the whist drives?'

Munroe didn't like his familiarity. He was stringing them along, telling them the 'truth' about the part of the evening and the events that he knew that they would check, and yet at the same time making light of it, all boys together.

He was either telling the truth, was innocent and had nothing to fear, or was cunning and clever.

They homed in on him. The Colonel's car, the one that had been involved in the fatal accident, it had been interfered with. Munroe swung round, 'Do *you* know how Charlie Somerville was killed?'

'I know the talk. Everybody does. The bonnet was gummed down. So that it'd fly up and kill some poor bugger.' He saw all too clearly where their logic was heading. 'Come on,' he said. 'You're not suggesting . . .'

'You *work* in a garage?'

'Yes, I work in a garage. On Saturday mornings. So what?'

'You'd know how to secure a bonnet with gum?'

'So would my granny!' he sneered.

The car was filled with cigarette smoke. The boy grimaced and wound down the window. It was stiff, rarely used.

Rees took the nice-guy part. His question was pointed, but the tone was conciliatory, 'You hit James Orme in the Horseshoe . . . ?'

'That hippy? He hit me. I just hit him back. He asked for it.'

'You've quite a temper, it seems,' said Munroe, watching him in the mirror.

'Come off it! That woman of his, no bra, she's putting herself about . . .'

Munroe swung round, his jaw set, his eyes blazing, and pushed his fingers into the boy's throat, 'Watch yourself, son, all right!'

Ryan pushed himself back in the seat, frightened. 'What's up with him?' he said to Rees.

Rees muttered to Munroe, 'Take it easy, John. Go on, Peter.'

'She's . . .' He looked up at Munroe, afraid of provoking him. '. . . you know, being *friendly* with the boys. We've had a win away. I was a bit pissed. We're all getting on fine except for her bloke who's just standing there miserable. Suddenly he lunges at me, and so I rolled him over and dropped him. He was a piece of piss. I could've killed him, easy.'

'You could have killed him, you say,' said Munroe.

'A manner of speaking,' said the boy sarcastically. 'He was nothing. These hippies, they're all love and peace, man. They don't know anything about scrapping.'

'And when Colonel Somerville runs you off his land, you're telling me you don't want revenge? Didn't take revenge? A little *something* to get your own back that went wrong?'

''Course not. He doesn't bother me. Louise and me, we can go anywhere. There's plenty more half-terms, lots of fields and barns. I know them all round here. She comes down here sometimes, when my old lady's out, slums it. She's all right, Louise.'

They told him to stay in the car and they sauntered up and down the little road of council houses.

'Nice boy,' said Munroe.

'Come on, John, he's all right. Bit rough, at least for round here, but not a killer.'

Munroe was not so sanguine. 'It didn't start off as a murder attempt, just a scare thing. The kind of thing he *could* do. What's his previous?'

'He's had a couple of fines . . . and he's on probation,' said Rees reluctantly.

'What for?'

'Assault,' said Rees.

'Oh yes?' said Munroe, smug.

'Down at the local dance. It's not unusual. That kind of thing's been going on for years round here. Local rivalries. Your village against mine. One week it's the flower show for the trophy, the next it's the choir competition, and now and again, on a Saturday night, the local youth bust one another's heads. It's nothing, I'm telling you, John. The kid's probably no better or worse than his dad and grandad were. There's just more of us bloody lot chasing 'em.'

Munroe was unimpressed by Rees's tolerance of local tribal customs. 'I think we should take him in, Tony. Put him under a bit of pressure. He's too obvious to leave out. And let's face it, we haven't exactly got a cell full of suspects down there.'

'I suppose it'll keep Nicklin off our backs for a bit. But we're wasting our time. He's a bit of a yob, that's all. And my missis'll kill me; she was born here and we've got Llandrinio in the semi-final of the Cup next week. He can confess to anything but he's coming out to play in that one!'

'Fair enough,' said Munroe.

They took the boy back into the house. Some of his jauntiness had disappeared. They explained to his mother that they were taking him to the station at Welshpool so that he could help them with their inquiries.

'For how long?' she asked, alarmed.

'Just for a while,' said Rees.

'As long as it takes,' added Munroe ominously.

The boy went up to his room with Rees to get a jacket. Against the wall, and below the Manchester United team posters and the huge portrait of George Best, was a drawing table.

Peter Ryan hadn't been an outstanding success at school, and when his art teacher had told divorced Mrs Ryan that the boy had real talent, could probably be a successful commercial or graphics artist, she had resolved to give him all the help that she could. His artist's bench had cost her a fortune.

Rees looked over the illustrations, designs and fanciful logos. At the top, to secure loose sheets of paper, was a malleable ball of white artist's rubber.

Rees went to the top of the stairs that ran up the house directly from the front door, and called, 'John, come up here a minute. You too, Mrs Ryan, please.'

CHAPTER TWENTY-NINE

At the therapy room in Shelton Hospital, Dorothea Somerville joined the little group and went to her seat. The red plastic chairs had no arms and she folded her hands demurely in her lap.

Dr Pickering smiled warmly, making eye-contact with each of the patients, and began to speak. In the next room, through the open door, the television flickered silently. From the kitchen beyond came the sound of detached, fragmented, normal life. Staff prepared food and washed cups; stainless steel surfaces clattered; incongruous laughter occasionally rang out.

As the doctor droned on, Dorothea started quietly to speak. At the first sound, three or four of the others looked across at her. The doctor was surprised. She had rarely spoken during her previous sessions.

She shivered involuntarily, 'I was cold. I'd been watching *Come Dancing*. Charles was in his room. Philip was out. He was in the Land-Rover.' There was a long pause.

'How did I know how to do it?

'A week before, my car was rattling. I stopped at a garage and asked them to check it.

'The man showed me how the bonnet hadn't shut properly, but he said that it was all right because of the safety-catch.' There was another long delay. Pickering looked very concerned. One of the patients began to gnaw at the skin on her fingers where the nails had once been.

'I went to Philip's car. I'd never sat in the driver's seat before. My feet wouldn't reach the pedals. I pulled the handle and the bonnet jumped up.

'Do you know the worst?' A tear rolled down her cheek

into the corner of her mouth. 'I used Charles's rubber. His drawing rubber. It gets too dirty in the end. He'd put it in his bin. And I saw it there. I wedged it into the catch and then I put some bits round the edges.'

She started to sob and rock and wrapped her arms around herself. The girl opposite drew rapidly on her cigarette so that the lighted end was one long piece of hot ash.

'I'd lived with his affairs for years. Nothing would have happened. If she hadn't sent me that thing. Why did she *do* that? She had him. But she taunted me. She was saying that she was still alive. She knew that mine had finished.

'It was horrible. Sophie had got it first. It was torn and chewed in the vestibule. It was horrible. The dog was sick. I cleared it up. Said nothing. But they couldn't do that to me. I was somebody once, too.'

Pickering came forward and sat in the chair next to her. 'It's good to talk,' he said, and gently put a hand on the woman's arm.

'Poor Charles,' she said. 'Poor, dear Charles,' and the teardrops blotted into her print dress.

When she was sedated and in her room, Pickering walked the grounds for an hour. He was deeply troubled.

Back in his office, he dialled Welshpool Police Station, 'Can I speak to Inspector Munroe, please?' he asked.

CHAPTER THIRTY

Munroe had to return to Birmingham the following day to tie up paperwork on a case that was coming to court the next week.

That evening, he drove back to his empty house in Handsworth. Kath had been back and there was a brief note on the table which ended with the address of her solicitor in offices in the Rotunda in Birmingham city centre. He wished it had been a cheaper address.

He opened drawers and cupboards at random. Most of her clothes were now gone. He wandered aimlessly from room to room. He could detect no particular significance in the things that she had left behind: it wasn't as if she had left every dress that he had ever bought her, nor taken every one that he had.

If he had known enough about fashion, what was in, what was hopelessly out, there might have been a clue there. But he didn't.

He went down into the cellar and stood and smelled its musty cool that he liked.

Upstairs, he opened a drawer in the dressing-table. There was some underwear there, and a swimming costume that he remembered from a holiday in Spain. In another one there were slips and cotton tops. In 'his' wardrobe there was a sad winter coat, some more dresses and a couple of skirts.

In the front room the bookshelves had big gaps where her books had been. In the kitchen, familiar utensils had gone.

From the sitting-room she had taken the standard lamp, an occasional table and the chairs from the three-piece suite.

She had gone to live with a man who owned a sofa but not a kitchen whisk or a pestle and mortar. He grinned to himself.

He went out to his car and brought in his bag and the record that the girl had given him. On the cover was the young Dylan; his face was defiant, angry, honest.

He put the record on the gramophone player and the boy started to sing about an encounter between 'a girl called Rita' and Tony Perkins. He lit a cigarette and sat on the back of the sofa with his feet on the cushions and listened. It was funny.

He turned the volume up and wandered again through all the downstairs rooms of the empty house.

Upstairs, he sat on the unmade bed in the half light of the early evening.

The words of the boy came up to him. It was a different, serious song, and the thin, insistent voice pleaded the refrain:

'Ah, but I was so much older then,
I'm younger than that now . . .'

He didn't turn off the gramophone; the record was still playing in the empty house as he headed up Soho Road, and out of Birmingham towards the motorway.

He drove up the lane in the absolute blackness of a country night, the twin headlights of the Zephyr piercing the dark and drawing him in.

Her van was there. He parked beside it.

There was a lamplight in the cottage and he knocked, very softly.

She drew open the door and they looked at one another. He wanted to speak, but had no idea what he was going to say. She stepped up to him, on tiptoes, and put her lips to his. He felt her little body against his and put his arms around her.

They made love straight away, wordlessly, on soft blankets that she spread before the glowing fire. Afterwards, they lay wrapped in one another's arms for a long time.

She kissed his neck and leaned across him and picked up her book from beside the hearth. He felt the weight of her breasts as she leaned across him.

The fire warmed his naked side.

'Listen,' she said softly, and began to read to him the two pages where Paul Morel makes love with Clara Dawes beside the River Trent.

When she reached the words '*He kissed her and gave way to joy*', he took the book from her, lay it down and folded her in his arms again.